SOUTHERN G ⌄⌄⌄

Best wishes

Jude

SOUTHERN GOLD

SURVIVAL AND DESIRE IN A RAW NEW LAND

JUDE THOMAS

SILVEREYE

AUCKLAND, NEW ZEALAND

Published by Silvereye Press.

Southern Gold is a work of fiction inspired by fact. The main characters and the plot are a product of the writer's imagination or are used fictitiously, and any resemblance to actual persons is coincidental. However, colonial Dunedin and the gold rush were very real, as were various events and some peripheral characters. Any misinterpretation or inaccuracies of historical detail is entirely unintended.

A catalogue record for this book is available from the National Library of New Zealand.

Author's website: judethomasauthor.com

Credits. Design: AnitaTaylorDesign.com. Southern Blue butterfly photo: ©rodmorris.co.nz. Author photo: imagesearch.co.nz

For my children Sarah, Miranda and Rory

Our vision was to create a new Utopia in this Colony, free from interference and freedom from filth. We brought superior morality to Dunedin, but now it is rapidly filling with drunkards, whores and bohemians. We, the old identity, are being swamped by this new iniquity.

Letter to the Editor, Otago Witness, 1862

PART ONE

CHAPTER ONE

⌁⌁⌁

Royal Terrace, Dunedin

1st January 1858

The garden party is in full swing and Donald Fraser scowls down upon it from his casement window. He has transported his family to the ends of the earth to carry out the Lord's work, and he doesn't approve of parties. Not only has he had to endure the first-footers last evening, but now – without more than a few hours' sleep – another day of torment has arrived. 'Heat-maddened crowds,' he groans; he cannot abide such displays of looseness. Yet here, right above his eyes, is a terrible beauty that clutches at his senses. Flashes of snowy white and blue-black feathers iridescent in the high sun, the winged lovers scooping and rising, embracing and parting – each on its own wild arabesque of desire. The

3

throb in Donald's groin borders on ecstasy. In spite of all else, in spite of what he believes the Lord commands, he thrills. It is pure torture, pure censure, pure sin. Or so it has been taught to Donald by his forefathers – kirk-embedded men of Edinburgh.

On the lawn, all is frivolity and it is a great day for it: not so warm as to make one excessively hot, but sufficient that most men are unfastened to their waistcoats. The women feel relaxed even in their crinolines, and the boldest children run barefoot on the soft lawn. Parasols, fans, tartan rugs, china tea sets, silver punch bowls and a string quartet. It is New Year's Day at 16 Royal Terrace, Dunedin.

The graceful timber house with its comfortable rooms, wide verandas and spacious garden has seen several such occasions, and each year they are increasingly anticipated by the Frasers and their guests. That is, by Elizabeth Fraser, her five daughters, and lately her small, sturdy son.

Although Donald does not care at all for these extravagant gatherings with the inevitable din of raucous children, he grudgingly allows Elizabeth to indulge in what she calls 'good works' by inviting the best of new society to these annual events. Dunedin is becoming quite a town, and he is mostly pleased by the breed and quality of the people increasingly populating it, many of them Scots, and of superior sensibilities. If only the new iniquity – Irish, Italians, Chinamen, Jews – could be sent back.

Elizabeth had been twenty when she met Donald.

4

Entranced by his brooding manner and simmering passion, she agreed to marriage soon thereafter. She came to know that Donald's primary passion was for the Lord, the Free Scottish Church, and the call to carry His Word and his seed to the new colony. His personal passions are so repressed she needs ingenuity to ignite them. And with much skill, Elizabeth sees to it that these are met while consoling Donald that he is indeed carrying out the Lord's work.

Elizabeth moves lightly about the carefully landscaped garden, offering smiles of greeting – and also laughter when her husband is not nearby. Donald does not much approve of laughter, although she knows he smiles slightly when he hears hers, and today is for summer and song. A group of guests are humming pretty English airs, and the Scots piper who ushered in luncheon is now florid with a wee bit more than the sun, aye.

Since arriving in New Zealand some ten years ago on the first immigrant ship, *John Wickliffe*, Elizabeth has made friends both within the stern church congregation and outside it. She has a grace and warmth that charms her acquaintances, and a soft invincibility that steers her through many situations. A new family that has moved in to Royal Terrace has strolled down to Number 16 in response to her invitation, still thanking a Providential Lord that their barque did not sink in horrifying seas a week out from Port Chalmers and that smashed china and crystal was their only casualty.

Many other acquaintances have arrived by carriage and there is much activity about the front lawn, gravel paths and shrubberies. Donald and Elizabeth's eldest daughter, Florence, walks with Alton Northey, and slides her eyes to meet his eagerness. Elizabeth smiles quietly; she feels that here may be the makings of a future proposal, although Florence is just seventeen and Alton is becoming quite a dandy.

Elizabeth has known a comfortable upbringing in Edinburgh, the loss of children and the love of more, the terror of the high seas and the challenge of a new land. Today she surveys her Dunedin garden with quiet satisfaction. Most of the cuttings and seedlings brought from Home on that long sea journey have transplanted well. And after years of back-breaking work clearing the native bush to the western boundary, the grounds are well established. Her only regret is that the azaleas are almost past their best for this day. With the chill spring and delayed summer they had bloomed late and she had hoped they would hold until this New Year's Day, but many of the petals now carpet the groves. Other than such a small inconvenience, the day is proving a success and Elizabeth is happy.

Donald Fraser tugs fiercely at his whiskers. Coming away inside, away from the crowd and the gaiety and especially the expectation of being a good host, was designed to gain some equilibrium. People wishing to bend his ear on trivial matters or make endless conversation about the weather aggravate him. Or to be truthful some, especially the females, terrify him. He grimly gives thanks that the garden event comes but once a year.

He allows Elizabeth to think that he doesn't know of her ruse as she calmly asserts it is their duty to be sociable for the greater good. But no doubt she is right, his beloved Elizabeth. It is only she who can persuade him that life on this earth is not just something to be borne by austerity of thought and in fear of the Lord, but to partake in with a modicum of happiness.

It was in pursuit of happiness of a kind that his spirit became awakened by the words of Edward Wakefield, campaigning for systematic colonisation of the heathen. But more importantly, he offered an opportunity to be free of the wrongs of society and the evils of the British church and state system. The new utopia, here in this new land, is what he had dreamed of. Land that for the first time was not tithed to any laird. Land where he would be charged with bringing Wakefield's vision to reality.

Yet Donald's mind is relentlessly torn. With a rigid, compassionless upbringing where work and prayer were the only acceptable activities, where guilt and punishment were constant cronies, he finds it extremely difficult to take pleasure in pleasure itself.

As he broods down over the garden Donald becomes aware again of the birds' erotic dance, and he groans in mortified pleasure. If only his feeble pencil sketches could catch the tui birds' lustre, those quivering snowy throat tufts – that ardent, unbridled freedom.

He reluctantly turns from the window and treads heavily downstairs to the front entrance of his grand home and garden. He breathes in deeply, forcing his face into genial lines. 'Dear fellow, madam, so honoured you could come to our wee gathering. We have been blessed with a bonnie day. Aye. Splendid, splendid.'

Alton Northey excuses himself from Florence and heads towards a group of fine young fellows like himself. He is already acquainted with bordellos and at nineteen he perceives himself to be quite the man. Any pretty girl is an opportunity for Alton. Rejection only sharpens his determination, and some fine ones at this colonial afternoon tea are surely ready for the chase. Dunedin is a crude place compared to his early memories of Edinburgh. Here it is muddy and raw, but bestowed with a light that sets his senses spinning. And what a day for it. He has spun from one female to the other, smoothly offering his arm to walk upon the gravelled pathways.

With no intention of having other than an agreeable time, he has gravely escorted Florence for a turn around the garden, using his charm and wit to transport her into an elevated state of mind. *Now this is one who will need somewhat more than gentle persuasion,* he lightly traces his arm about her sashed waist, *but her dowry could be handsome.*

Most of the guests are known to Alton as friends and acquaintances of his parents. Some, like the Frasers, were companions on the sea voyage many years ago when he was a boy; some old hands when he arrived; and yet others are recent arrivals.

Alton's reverie is broken by shrill giggles from the azalea

grove and he moves towards the drifts of pink, white and mauve. Eveline Fraser has been nabbed by her small brother, William, and her full white dress is in disarray. Ecstatic after ten minutes of hiding and seeking, three-year-old William stumbles from the shrubbery and with a high shout, staggers away on his fat toddler legs.

Alton is transfixed by the lovely glowing thing that is Florence's sister Evie, fulsome as a ripe peach. Good Lord, how and when did this happen? The last time they met she was a child in a pinafore, and now –! His blood pulses. He is magnetised.

Evie gasps to find Alton viewing her torn drawers, but he eases the moment by reaching for a flower, murmuring about delicate petals and firm stamens. She is transfixed by his intense amber eyes ringed with smoky blue – slanted eyes that she has always thought to be strangely exotic.

Now he's so close, and so hotly breathing into her neck, that Evie believes she must be on fire. Her back is melting into the bracts and her legs are weak but he catches her and holds her close. He whispers her name, telling her she is lovelier than a summer's day. His body is hot too, and he is pressing and pressing, hard and unstoppable. Evie is engulfed with a wild surge that surely is ecstasy. She opens herself to the moment, and the moment's exquisite pain is overcome by the thrill, and it is delicious.

The encounter is so brief and intense and wonderful she hardly can think of the botany lesson he began. 'Oh!' She shudders with delight. 'Oh! Lovely – lovely!' Then with a gasp and shudder the sensation fades and is soon gone.

And Alton is gone too, mumbling like a spent fool, fleeing the grove of petals and stamens as fast as little William. Evie breathlessly wrests her dishevelled petticoats to order so as not to receive a scolding from Mother.

'William? William! Hide quickly, for I'm coming to find you. Coming ready or not!'

CHAPTER TWO

———∿∿∿———

1st September 1858

Friday nights in the Fraser household sees the children, with the exception of William, staying up one hour later than the rest of the week.

Summer had faded into crisp days that saw the garden's harvest make way for the winter vegetables, and all the outdoor activities attended to before the Antarctic air stream flowed onto the land. Then came the frosts and the sleet and the chilling draughts that Donald and Elizabeth are accustomed to from their upbringing. And yet here in New Zealand each wonderful mild summer continues to trick their notice, so that the subsequent southern winters of their new homeland always surprise them. This is the first day of a new antipodean spring and while it is still sharply grey, it is also full of promise.

Donald allows himself two drams of whisky on a Friday

evening; otherwise he maintains one and a half. The Sabbath is, of course, for abstinence and for seeking forgiveness from the Lord.

The evening meal, still known as supper although it is now being called tea by those in the outer districts, is inevitably cold mutton cut at table with silent dignity by Donald. Each plate also receives a single boiled potato, sized accordingly; it is unwise to indulge in rich food after four o'clock. Mustard is mixed in a silver pot and passed around as the only accompaniment. Then it is into the drawing room, where charades are mimed with flapping and giggling, recitations are presented with earnestness, and songs are sung with sweet innocence. Donald does not enjoy such nonsense, but Elizabeth insists her girls acquire good social graces and become accomplished. Sunday sermons are for admonishing the flock in their sinful ways, and no songs are sung, but Elizabeth maintains that entertainment on Fridays should include music to gladden the soul.

Against his ingrained sense of doom and solitude, Donald allows his wife and daughters this liberty, but songs must be suitable – quiet and gentle. Anything of excess is not to be considered; his whole Presbyterian life has been bound up in avoiding excess. Certainly no rollicking reels or whisky-sodden wha-hae.

Elizabeth favours 'Drink to Me Only with Thine Eyes', and Donald's cheeks pinken when she seeks out his during her modest performance. She is also fond of 'Scarborough Fair', and her eyes moisten as she remembers her own English mother so far away, and whom she will probably never see again.

One of Eveline's current favourites is 'Skye Boat Song'; she is in love with the notion of the lad who is born to be king speeding to safety on a bonnie boat. She also wishes to sing 'Comin' thro' the Rye' but Father will not have it because of the reference to kissing.

Florence's clear voice caresses 'Sweet Afton', and she has recently learned what she skilfully calls 'Marble Halls'. Florence pictures the vision of forbidden love; Donald does not know that the aria comes from an opera about a Bohemian gypsy girl. Such connotations would cause a frightful stirring in his withers. But he keeps his thoughts steadfast and hears his girls through their tomfoolery. His fingers are laced firmly together across his tartan waistcoat, although his errant thumbs revolve slowly around each other, back and forth, forth and back. When each daughter has done her piece he nods – done, accomplished. Donald never utters praise. Occasionally he will pat-pat an outstretched arm. Mother, alone, with her merry eyes and sideways glances at her husband, claps and cries out, 'Well done, my dear, well done.'

This Friday night is still chilly away from the fire's short reach, but they are warmed by their exertions.

'Goodnight, Mother; goodnight, Father,' say Florence and Eveline in unison. They embrace Elizabeth then peck at Donald's brow. It is nine o'clock.

The two eldest daughters are the last to depart for their beds, following a strict routine where baby William returns to the nursery first; Jean and Isobel aged seven and eight go reluctantly at the chime of eight o'clock. Mary Beatrice, deciding two years ago on her tenth birthday that she should be called May, is happy to dance out of the drawing room one half hour later. This leaves Evie and Florence, some three years apart at fourteen and seventeen, but closely bonded and not wishing to be separated in the evening ritual. Florence would rather retire earlier with Evie and have time before blowing out their candles to brush her younger sister's thick, straight hair. Evie, in return, treasures the moments when Florence can whisper about her young gentlemen admirers.

'Goodnight, daughters. Be sure to say your prayers and ask God's forgiveness for your sins.' Donald Fraser speaks these commandments on a regular basis.

It is warm in the parlour, but once they have left that cosy room the temperature slaps them at two degrees above freezing. Dashing towards the stairs, the sisters know their beds will have received hot stones to warm their feet.

Then Eveline reels on the landing, gasps and clutches her belly – too much contraband pudding earlier in the day no doubt, left over in the pantry.

'Evie, are you unwell?' Florence twists on the upper stairs to see her younger sister bent double.

'Yes, no – just a little indigestion, I think,' laughs Eveline, climbing the remainder of the flight more slowly.

The stairs at Royal Terrace are a gracious feature, with imported heart-oak for treads, but gleaming kauri for the balustrade. When the house was being built Elizabeth insisted on using native timbers as much as possible. And Elizabeth's inspiration has proved well, as usual; the kauri glows like polished amber, modest, yet gracious.

'Evie, I think you are getting much too plump, and this makes you out of breath. You know, these past weeks I have wondered if fifteen is too long to wait before getting you into stays.'

'Stays! Those frightful, boned cages – I don't know how you manage, Floss!' gasps Evie.

'It isn't a question of managing. It's just proper. And it gives one the silhouette required to become a woman,' replies Florence earnestly. 'Honestly, Evie, it is so important to show a small waist – you'll see.'

Evie gasps again but regains her composure. She will be a young woman soon. She will put up her hair and lengthen her skirts, but she will not give in to inconveniences. She undresses quickly and slides into a thick flannel nightgown, and the sisters kneel at their high beds to say the Lord's Prayer in rapid unison; the floor rugs give futile warmth to their knees. Once in her feathered bed, feet upon the hot stone vessel and layers of eiderdowns comforting her, Evie relaxes into a cosy trance.

Until a sharp pain makes her intake her breath. Then it happens again.

'Bother, why did I eat all that pudding earlier, Floss? And I had some plums too.'

Twenty minutes later a similar dagger seems to plunge into her lower back, then ease off, and she floats back into sleep. Once more the agony wakens her, fiercer and deeper.

'Florence, Floss, *oh*! Oh sister, it's a terrible pain!'

'I shall run to get Mother!' cries Florence.

'No, no, please don't – you know Father will be furious to have his evening interrupted. I am sure it's just those plums and tomorrow it will have passed!' begs Eveline between gasps. 'Please, please don't go down.'

But then a violent wave returns and Evie moans through gritted teeth until it subsides. Ten minutes later it overtakes her once again. Then again. And again, thrusting and raking like a maddened serpent. Now Florence rejects her sister's pleas as she throws a wrap around her nightgown and dashes down the stairs. Mother and Father are preparing to depart the drawing room for their own night's rest before a busy Saturday spent directing the maid and ensuring all is achieved before the Lord's Day on which there will be no cooking, cleaning or work of any kind.

'Mother, come quickly. Evie is very indisposed and –'

'Wheesht!' Donald rises. 'How dare you burst in without knocking! Calm yourself, Florence and do not raise your voice in this way. Your sister has eaten too much, as usual, and is probably out of sorts.'

'No, no, Mama, please do come directly! Evie is very ill!'

Leaving Donald to puff and snort about females – everywhere females, just to irk him – Elizabeth snatches the hallstand candelabra and surges towards the room that Florence and Evie have shared for many years.

Once a nursery, it is now transformed into a young ladies' boudoir, the walls papered with a pattern of soft grey trellis and dusky rambling roses. The grey jacquard curtains are full and graceful. A chaise padded with mauve brocade invites leisure by the western wall; a matching chair and inlaid table are set before the window. The twin bedheads are intricately inlaid with rosewood and mahogany. Fat mauve eiderdowns enhance the room's grace.

But the covers on Eveline's bed are in disarray. Her legs are awry. And there is a gaping sphere between Evie's pale thighs and she is screaming and screaming and screaming. The rapidly escalating pain has given way to an unbearable, searing agony. 'Oh, Mother, Flossie, help me, help me! I am surely being split in two!'

Elizabeth and Florence are transfixed by shocked revulsion – Elizabeth with dawning recognition of the impending event, Florence in terror of the gleaming wetness, and both knowing it must surely be a nightmare.

Eveline is pushing, pushing, gasping, shrieking. At last, with a piercing, primeval howl and a pulsing gush of crimson, she expels a sodden lump. It is blue and still.

And then the tiny thing moves. It utters the faintest croak. The newborn jerks its scrawny limbs and establishes a high, indignant wail.

CHAPTER THREE

3rd September 1858

'Slattern! Trollop!' roars Donald. 'She must arise and be gone!'

'But, my dear, we must think carefully,' implores Elizabeth.

The birth of Eveline's baby has delivered a seismic jolt to life at Royal Terrace.

Eveline has been confined to the room she has shared with Florence for many years. Florence has been removed to share another room with May, and despite all coaxing she remains withdrawn. May has been told that Florence has a case of nerves and must stay quiet, and to please take her noise elsewhere. Jean, Isobel and baby William continue their daily routine with Donald's sister and governess.

Donald and Elizabeth have spent two days alternately clinging to one another and disputing what is to happen now. The doctor has not been called. No one has come or gone from the house except the butcher's boy at the servants' gate.

'I'm sure Doctor Prichard would be discreet and find a placement for a childless couple,' pleads Elizabeth.

'I cannot abide the notion of his involvement,' shouts Donald.

'Then perhaps sister Prudence who lives such an isolated life in the Maungatua hills might be persuaded. I know she loves company, especially when the men are away droving, and a baby might – '

'I will not hear of it!'

'Then I believe there is an orphanage up north where the nuns take in foundlings, so perhaps – '

'Papists! Never will my family have such a blemish upon its future! But no, that child is not of my family, never again. Whore! Strumpet!' And Donald staggers to the chesterfield, for his legs will not hold him up.

'Donald, my dear, we must think clearly, and pray to our Lord to help us find a way.'

'Pray? Pray, Mrs Fraser? I am at a loss to know why the Lord has forsaken me and my prayers!'

'Forsaken you? *Forsaken you?* Donald, for shame!'

'You dare speak against me, woman? For shame yourself!' Donald leaps from his prone position as if to strike his wife.

Immediately he stops, his arm suspended high. Never in his life has he struck a woman, although aye, there are many who do. Many who consider women, wives in general, to be worthy of striking in order to make them know the path of righteousness, the way of submitting to the man who is the head of the household and to be obeyed. But Donald vowed from an early age, after witnessing the beatings of his father upon his mother whom he revered, that he would never ever strike another, let alone a woman and especially a wife.

He crumples towards Elizabeth's arms. 'Oh, wife, if only the Lord would strike me down,' he cries, then almost immediately regains composure and draws himself up. 'But no, it is she who has conspired with the devil! She must be cast out!'

'No, no! Please, my dear husband, this is your beloved daughter who has been wronged.'

Donald's wild eyes focus on yet another internal combustion. 'Wronged? *Wronged!* And if I ever catch the scoundrel who has wronged her I shall shoot him immediately. Or I shall shoot myself! Or I shall shoot her! But first I must find the brute, the mongrel, the – '

'Calm yourself, Donald, we must be calm.'

'Calm – yes, yes, let us pray for calm amidst the storm, let us pray to be relieved of this abomination. Let us pray, Elizabeth!'

And so the perpetual, revolving tableau continues. Donald seems alternatively to have lost his wits, or become focused on retribution, or sink into his chair in a deep state of melancholy. He will not leave the drawing room; will not take respite in his bed. Elizabeth moves around the house, endeavouring to keep regularity with her children, and reassuring the household that all will be well directly.

Elizabeth visits Eveline and her infant on the hour, and gently guides the routine. Eveline's budding breasts have been bound and her body cleansed with carbolic soap, something Elizabeth's women friends have discreetly discussed as being a valuable item not only for the kitchen. The scrap of a thing is sucking well on the bottle and Evie seems to be either in a state of unfathomable daze or blissful dote. Perhaps, thinks Elizabeth, she believes it is a doll.

The window curtains are drawn, with only a chink for daylight. The heavy door drape is pulled across, and an enormous draught-stop pushed against the gap to muffle the inevitable newborn cries.

'Baby will soon be leaving,' mother says quietly to daughter.

'Baby leaving?' Eveline is vague.

'And it shall not be spoken of again.'

'Not be spoken of, not be spoken of ... '

It is noon on the third day and Elizabeth once again descends the stairs. She is exhausted with lack of sleep. Exhausted with worry about Evie. About Florence, who still wakes screaming and sobbing, then falls back into a swoon. Exhausted with Donald's refusal to agree to any of her suggestions of dealing with the situation. She clutches the landing banister and squeezes her eyes against the world, against the newborn, and against Donald's increasingly demented moods.

Clearly, it would be sensible to engage Doctor

Pritchard's knowledge of these things and find the babe a home with some deserving couple. This, she is confident, would not be the first time he would have been thus engaged. But Donald will not hear of it.

Alternatively, it would not be difficult for Elizabeth to increase the padding of her body and dress, and infer she is with child once more. William is three now, and it would be perfect timing to have a new one in the family. In a couple of months or so she could be confined and delivered of a bonnie wee girl. This ruse, she is aware, would not be the first time that a baby has to all intents and purposes emerged from a convenient womb. Donald is appalled by the hint of this notion; he has never heard of such a thing.

But then again, it would be normal that Evie goes away under the guise of visiting some friends up north or down south. A plan where the child could be left to grow in safe surroundings and be brought up as a little cousin, or some such. A plan where she, too, is away from all this agitation. Where – oh, wait! Thank you, Lord! That is the Plan!

As if in slow motion, Elizabeth regains her composure, raises her head and squares her shoulders. She will not stand it a moment longer, this hiatus of all that is sensible. She firmly descends to confront a startled Donald.

'Donald Fraser, you are master of this house, it is true. But in the absence of your clear reason I am mistress of its future. You will listen to me and be done with it. Your options are clear.'

'I refuse to be lectured! Be gone, woman.'

'I shall not be gone, and you should not dare to suggest

it. Now *you* shall listen. Tomorrow I shall leave this house with all our children and – and – stay away. Indefinitely,' she extemporises. 'Or, preferably, I will leave with Eveline and proceed to ensure our granddaughter – yes, Donald, our own granddaughter! – will be welcomed and loved, for none of this is of her doing, the poor child. I shall take charge, and this is what is to be done. No, please stay seated, Mr Fraser, and hear me out.'

But Donald cannot comprehend the woman. Leave? Stay away?

'I shall write immediately to sister Caroline asking her to assist us,' Elizabeth continues relentlessly. 'If I send the letter at first light tomorrow, the horseman should reach Outram by sunset and with speed, he should arrive at the house before dark. Then my dear sister will have time to read my letter and recover her wits before we arrive.'

A revised plan comes to her mind. 'But wait, here it is: I shall send Evie and the babe on by the earliest bullock wagon the following morning and they should be there by evening. The bullocks may be changed at Mosgiel so there should be no delay. Evidently the track is much improved. And then, husband, I shall make the same journey directly I have organised this household. There! It is settled. Caroline is steady and reliable, and the boarding house she runs is very respectable, she writes me so. Comings and goings are normal, so nothing will seem amiss.'

Donald looks further dazed. Bullocks? Comings and goings?

'But here comes the next part of the plan before we

return. We shall find a foster mother for the babe, some kind woman whom Caroline can vouch for, and whom we shall reward for the promise to bring her up in the fullness of time. And in that time we shall treasure this strategy. Husband, our dear Eveline and her infant have been sorely done by, but now we must do the best thing. We *must* act.'

'But, I shall not allow – I – you – ' Donald feebly endeavours to respond.

For the first time in her married life, Elizabeth lifts her head defiantly and stares resolutely into her husband's desperate eyes. 'I have spoken.'

CHAPTER FOUR

4th September 1858

It is first light, raw and bleak. Elizabeth gives a final tuck to the heap of rugs covering Eveline and the picnic hamper, with the tiny one swaddled in a paisley shawl and wedged into its woven bed. Evie's eyes are bright now and with layers of woollen garments and Elizabeth's own fur cloak, they are wrapped up tight against the biting cold. The driver stamps on thickly-frosted ground and acknowledges his instructions to drive with care – but with no waste of time – to her sister's home some fifty miles southwest.

'Be brave, Evie, keep the little one warm, and Aunt Caroline will be waiting. You should arrive before dark. Then I shall arrive in a few days' time.'

The driver and his two bullocks are not familiar with Royal Terrace – they usually commence and end their journey at Forbury – but Elizabeth has swiftly managed to find a man who would come over the hill to collect his charges before making the journey across the Taieri Plains. He has little to say. His services are regularly called upon to drive goods hither and yon, and he is well paid and has good sustenance in his belly as a result. He wishes to know no more.

'Farewell, my dear. Just rest yourself as much as possible with the jolts, and soon you shall be with your aunt. And then the Lord will guide us in how best to give the baby up.'

Eveline clutches the fur cloak to her face as the wagon starts to move on.

The transport slowly traverses Royal Terrace and takes to the high road that will ultimately descend to the south. The animals plod at their one solid, unswerving pace. Evie is cosy under the woollen rugs, and she is getting warmer and warmer.

Give the baby up. Give the baby up. Her mother's final words pulse, surge and then violently break through her senses and she is suddenly chilled.

'I say, I say! Stop stop stop! I say, driver! Stop this wagon!' Suddenly she is alive with passion. The driver cannot hear with his greatcoat collar up and his ears muffed against the chill breath of dawn, but becomes aware of thumping and agitation from his load, and reins in his beasts.

'Set me down! I must get down – set me down this instant!'

'But, miss, my instructions are – '

'No, no, it is not to be so! You must help me down!'

'I dare not, miss. I must deliver you – '

'Deliver, phooey! Deliver me here at once, I say!' Eveline draws on her fourteen years' knowledge of command.

'But, miss, the lady has paid me – '

'Here's an extra payment.' She thrusts her pouch with its guinea at the bewildered man. 'Take it and be gone, but let me down now! I say: *now*!'

With lumbering awkwardness, the driver unloads his wagon's cargo: the bundle of girl, fur and hamper. She refuses the blankets. He stares at the road from whence he has come and to which he is headed. He stares at his purse. Slowly, uncertainly, he shrugs, climbs back onto his plank, and does not look back. 'Gedd-up,' he growls at the bullocks.

Eveline draws in a deep breath of freezing air. It scalds her lungs and elevates her senses. She cannot feel her finely booted feet on the frozen ground. Determinedly she draws the cloak tight around the hamper; her baby is asleep in its little bed and she shall never, ever let it go. She shall dress it and feed it and play with it. She shall sing 'Speed Bonnie Boat' to it. She shall keep it and it shall never, ever be Given Up.

She meanders along the top road, a trail of fur and fever. She drifts along Royal Terrace, and on into Maori Hill. It is dark, but the sky seems to be on fire; in reality is beginning to lighten with a cruel, icy wash.

From the depths of the picnic hamper comes a gentle mewling.

Otago Witness, Monday 6th September, 1858
TAIERI FLOODS

Flash flooding of the Taieri River has resulted in drownings. This took place on Saturday 4th Inst., after the Plain was flooded by torrential rain in the upper reaches of the River. A Witness said he lost much Stock due to the flood. He said he was caught short, due to the fact the River rose so rapidly in frightful surges. He claimed that he might face Bankruptcy.

Another Witness said he saw a Bullock Team and Wagon being swept away while attempting to ford the River, some twenty miles south of Outram. No sightings have yet been recorded of any Survivor, nor Goods on board. It is assumed that All have been swept rapidly downstream and out to sea.

CHAPTER FIVE

Alf Maguire shudders, blows on his hands and knots his woollen scarf tighter. Dolly stomps and snorts, and they both breathe hoary puffs into the grey light. He slaps her affectionately before heaving himself onto the creaky cart, and settles onto the box seat as she slowly clomps along the side alley and onto the earthen road. Spring has officially started but the ground is still frozen with treachery.

Maclaggan Street is the arse-end of Dunedin town, but a sweet home to Alf these past nine-some years since he and Meg arrived at Port Chalmers after that long voyage from London with hardly a shilling between them. But there was no doubt it was to be a better life. Alf, come over from Belfast to London as a lad and whose family hadn't found it much better, and Meg, come up from Kent as a maid, fell in love and wed. They moved in with Alf's brothers and their families but crowding, disease, little income, and finally the lure of free travel to New Zealand drove them on. They fitted the criteria, paid their hard-earned pound and emigrated on the HMS *Ajax* in the northern autumn of 1848. After a turbulent four-month journey, they progressed steadily and a mere two years later were ready to build their own home. Using their wits, and timber that was plentiful and free, they began to prop up a sturdy shack, then expand and modestly furnish it room by room to become Maguire's Private Hotel. It is humble but clean and brings in a good living due largely to Meg's reputation of no-nonsense motherliness, rich mutton stews and clean bedding.

Every morning except Sunday is the same for Alf. At daybreak he hugs the comatose form of his wife, rises from the bed knowing she is unconcerned about the twang of bedsprings, and lowers his feet to the rag rug. He pulls on the same attire day after day, even though Meg boils up a storm of laundry three times a week to keep up with the guests. He can't be doing with fresh clothes other than of a Sunday; Meg has enough to do without his extras. So today's attire is the same as yesterday and the day before: woollen combinations, flannel shirt and serge suit complete with waistcoat. The suit was firstly his brother's, then his own marriage getup, and now his work attire, patched and darned as maybe. And always the woollen scarf tied neatly at his throat. All tidy and well pressed; just because he is a collector, there is no need to lower his standards. He leaves a topcoat in the cart in case of rain. Otherwise day in, day out except for Sundays, it is the same getup as he goes about his business.

Sometimes Mungo comes with him, but during these frosty mornings his raggedy doggy form stays curled up in front of the coal range, still slightly warm from the night's banking.

Alf usually heads downhill towards town, always hopeful of finding discarded or lost articles from the previous day and evening. 'Let's see what lies abandoned for us today, my lovely,' he always imparts towards Dolly's thick neck. Leather gloves – pairs for selling, singles for other uses. Silver flasks, fob watches, jewellery, fur wraps – these are what he really wants, and if people are so careless as to leave or drop them, so be it. Alf always holds valuable articles for twenty days before disposing of them, checking Lost & Found in the *Otago Witness*, hopeful of a reward. Then it's off to hawk his wares to Ben Solomon, or into his own small workshop beside the scullery for restyling or repairing. Most of the time the day's collection is more mundane articles, dropped or thrown out: bits and bobs that come in handy. He is adept at converting one thing into another: inventing, altering and creating a silk purse from a sow's ear before peddling it for a copper or two.

His route is bordered by High Street to the south, Princes Street to the east and Stuart Street to the north. And to the west, the City Rise is all his territory. Alf stoutly guards his implicit right to these blocks south of the Bell Hill cutting, which is slowly being widened and lowered to allow passage of transport between the two parts of the town. His route in and out of the rutty lanes and wider roads takes him until well after midday, depending on how many times he stops and how much dust has been rained into mud. He smiles at the thought of the venerable city planners from the Home country, designing streets of such geometrical beauty on paper – contrary to the reality of carving such detail into the hinterland's steep slopes.

Today, for no reason except that it would be a change and a change is as good as a rest, Alf swishes at Dolly and guides her left at Rattray Street instead of dropping down to the usual Princes Street, then heads up the incline towards York Place. Some servants of the big houses leave items outside the back gates. A few of them scorn his trade and shout obscenities, as if their service to the wealthy makes them fit to look down upon those who are their own master, like himself. But mostly folk treat him with respect, as he does them.

Alf hums to himself as they plod along. Not much luck so far, only a brass knob off a carriage and a pair of broken spectacles, but let's press on further up the Rise and see what the day brings. The uphill pull is taxing Dolly's bones and he will get down soon and walk beside her. For after Meg, Doll is the most precious thing to Alf.

Then he sees a lump, probably a blanket, discarded in the middle of the road some way up ahead. Most likely fallen off a carriage taking some people home from their evening at cards, or a ball. Alf knows the ones who live up the Rise have different pastimes than himself, despite their similar aspirations of a new life in a new country. Dolly clops steadily upward, her breath steaming in the frosty air.

'Whoa, Doll, that's my sweet. And what have we here?' Alf draws closer and looks down at the heap of cloth and for a split second, it moves. Perhaps a stray dog finding shelter?

He gets off the cart and bends to examine the goods. 'Bugger me days – a fur coat, quite a find of a morning.'

Dolly nudges the mound.

'Strike me pink, a nice little boot!' *But wait – it's on a foot!* 'Oh, bloody hell – has there been a murder?'

And then a noise – not quite a mew, nor a squawk. A husky, kittenish squeak. And another. Alf reaches forward, and with trepidation lifts the edge of the fur to expose a picnic hamper with its lid loose. He cautiously lifts it. Two orbs stare out, unblinking.

'Gawd save us, it's – it's a babby!' Alf gawps. 'Alive, although how is it possible on this bitter morning! And here's the poor mother – she's frozen to death!' Or maybe not quite?

Alf half-straightens and looks about in a mix of caution and irritation, for this surely must be some silly prank? But the day is still dim and only a dog's bark further up the hill cuts through the early morning miasma. He swings onto the cart to grab his old coat from within the box seat, jumps down, and roughly swaddles the basket. As he lifts it carefully to his chest, the new-old eyes stare back at him, and Alf feels an overwhelming wave of premonition.

Then he collects himself, climbs rapidly back up onto the cart and places the bundle gently into the seat's cavity. Leaps back down again and widely spreads his arms to encircle the lady within the fur – *Gawd save us, it's not a lady at all, blimey it's just a girl!* – shoulders her up onto the cart and covers her with his own knee rugs.

'There will be no more collecting directly, Alf me old

china, we must make speed to Meg. She'll know what to do – gedd-up Doll!'

The horse eases the load downhill and Alf shivers with concern as he urges her towards Maclaggan Street.

Meg hears his shout and hastens into the backyard, still in her nightgown and thick shawl. She rises at six, one half-hour after Alf has crept downstairs, and after previously feigning sleep. She can't be doing with kisses and carry-on of a morning, and this small sham has been part of her ten-year married life – eight of them in their own little boarding house. That is, the accommodation that she calls a private hotel, so as to attract respectable folk rather than itinerants and dubious characters.

And here now is Alf, dragging Dolly and bellowing to come quick. Is something wrong with the animal, and if so what is she to do about it? She has more to do than nurse a horse. Or if it is a substantial find, why involve her at this time of the morning? But there is something urgent about Alf today; he is shaking and gasping. He draws her to the cart, and to the fur-wrapped bundle.

'My Lord, whatever have you got there, Alfie? What have you done?'

'I done nothing, Meg, she was on the bloomin' road! Dead, I thought, but no. I believe she is a young lady, and almost alive!'

'Then hurry, you foolish man, don't stand around dithering. Bring her down and into the warm. I was just stoking up the range!'

Meg prepares to run back indoors, already shivering in

the raw air, and stumbles over Mungo's yelping, circular trajectory.

'But Meggy, look too, there's a bundle, a bob, bab ba – '

'For goodness' sake, man, come in with the – '

'A babby!' Alf spits it out, half-demented with the thought of it.

Meg turns and gazes incredulously as her husband delicately brings forth the hamper and she gasps again. 'Oh, oh Alf, whatever have you done?'

'I done nothing, Meg – they was on the road, I tell you! I thought they was just an old blanket, then I thought: No, Alf my son, this is more than a blanket, this is a fur and it will be another one to clean up and store and take care in laying out and calculating how to advertise it to best advantage in the Lost and Found column, like – '

'Great heavens, man, stop mithering! Give it over to me. Deary-deary me, whatever have you done?'

Meg draws a deep, shuddering breath and composes herself. She hasn't endured her whole life of being sharp and keen and having the wits about her to be contradicted now by this peculiar to-do. She carefully receives the hamper and glances back up into her husband's wide, fearful eyes. Then she looks down at the foundling's face, and for a flashing moment is seized with the same emotion that struck Alf. A surge of shock and awe that sends a wave of chills over her body. Chills that are nothing to do with the rawness of the morning.

She turns back into the kitchen and eases the hamper onto the sturdy pine table that serves all manner of purposes, then wrenches open the coal range's door, hurls a log into the embers and opens the damper wide. The range is only a few months old and is Meg's pride and joy after cooking over an open fire these past years. Saved up, they did – well, she saved it; Alf just handed over his coin and she did the calculations and ordered it to be brought over from Home. Such a contraption at first, but a boon with her constant stream of paying guests who need hearty meals.

Alf follows, carrying Eveline's limp form, and with the benefit of only one look from his wife, lays the stranger on the hearth mat. The small kitchen is regaining its warmth. Meg and Alf don't speak. They hold their hands to their face, over their mouth, over their eyes; they look at each other, and they look back to the lady – no, still just a girl – and the infant.

Then Meg whispers, 'Oh, Alf, Alf! How? Where – ?'

But they are not to know from where Evie has tottered, within sight of the big gates of Royal Terrace. Not to know how, with increasing delirium, her world seemed bathed in a triumphant blaze of colour. Or how long she stumbled on until the blaze faded into blackness. Or when she crumpled and folded dreamlike onto the icy ground, onto to the wrapping that would provide salvation for a time. Until an old nag gently nudged the shroud.

For three days and nights Meg nurses her acquisitions with a tenderness that flows naturally. Although she has no child of her own – a constant sorrow mitigated by a strong and loving personality – she helped her Ma birth several. And this little mite is surely weeks short of a full term.

'Young Lady' is what they call this mother – just a girl, but a maiden no more. She hasn't opened her eyes much less spoken, but her garments are of fine silk and soft woollen and kid leather, not to mention that full fur cloak, and these set her apart from the likes of themselves. Her fever is starting to come down, the intimate bathing is soothing her body, she is absorbing a drop or two of broth under her tongue, and her milk is starting to leak naturally now that the bindings are removed. *We will need to see about that – it needs to flow or it needs a brew of sage to stop it*, Meg notes.

Young Lady has been lifted onto the narrow corner settle and protected by a timber contraption hurried up by Alf to guard against falling when – *and if*, he notes only to himself – she wakes.

'Little One' is what they call the scrap at first. And oh my Lord, wrapped in a finely woven shawl. Looking just like a doll, but becoming demanding after the first day of startled survival in the warm kitchen. Meg finds an oval bottle left behind by a guest and boils it for ten minutes in a pan with a slug of carbolic until the glass shines and the dropper is spotless. Milk from their gentle cow is skimmed and scalded and diluted, and after a cranky start Little One takes most of what is offered. Roars again at having her warm and pungent napkin interfered with, then sleeps long and sweet, tucked into her hamper bed.

There are only four paying guests at present – a husband and wife come in from the country to await the arrival of family immigrants at Port Chalmers, plus a couple of single gentlemen. They don't venture into the kitchen, and at any rate, Young Lady and Little One are none of their affair. Alf and Meg have decided – or rather, Meg has decided and Alf naturally agrees – that Young Lady should give them her own account when she comes to her senses. That is, before any other investigations are made. Meg knows deep in her waters that discretion is the best way to go about things.

CHAPTER SIX

Eveline is returning, slowly and intermittently. She has no knowledge of her days in a coma on the kitchen settle, nor the three subsequent nights that she has been carried upstairs to a mattress at the foot of Alf and Meg's bed. Through a dense fog, like the blanket that frequently shrouds Otago Harbour on winter mornings, she gauges sounds and movements. But where do they come from? Perhaps she will turn back home, but it is warm and peaceful and who wants to leave such a sensation? Then again, it is too wearisome to push against the fog. It comes, and it goes.

Eventually the pall thins, her eyes flutter and vaguely she sees a woman's form; it must be Mother. Evie is cosy and just wants to close her eyes again, and she returns to a dream state. But after a while Mother is sobbing – oh, Mother, what is amiss? Sobbing and banging a pot. But how peculiar; Mother doesn't bang pots. And her mouth is open in a scream but no noise comes out. And Florence is joining her distress. But wait – now she is humming and poking the fire.

Slowly the sounds are becoming more defined. The heaviness is lifting and the cloud dispersing. She is staring at the back of a woman working away before a coal range, lifting lids and stirring, letting the aroma of lamb stew waft about, and bending down and removing a large dish from the oven. Holding it aloft with sacks about her hands, before placing it on a table. Saying, 'That should fill their bellies tonight.' And turning, with her sack dropping down onto her apron strings, and saying in a definite way but without surprise, in a voice that is not like Mother's, 'Bless her, she is wakening.'

Eveline regains her senses and recollects a few details at a time. She cannot remember how she came to be here in this busy kitchen. But little by little she recalls, her awareness reversing in small stages. The shame of an event beyond her comprehension. The sobbing of her mother. The horror in the eyes of her sister. The appalling pain and the pushing, pushing, pushing out of a slippery thing. The shouting of her father. And returning again to the shame.

Now she finds herself here in this kitchen, with a sleeping baby alongside her own makeshift bed.

Meg takes Eveline's hands and says in her straightforward but gentle way, 'You were found on the road, miss, half frozen. Tell us your name, my dear, and nothing more until you say so.'

'Evie. Eveline. Eveline F – ' and she stops short. Everything is swirling in her head and who is this woman? Maybe she has stolen me? But no, not this homely, soft woman with her kindly eyes. And yet, I must not say, for it is – and again anguish encases her – *it is not to be spoken of.*

Then Evie remembers the silent, frosty morning air that enveloped her when Mother opened the front door one morning. When was that? And how bone-chilling it was, and the path crunched as they made their way to the wide iron gate. Evie has always loved that gate, so intricate and yet so serene, and she has often run her fingers over the rods and hoops and the entwined thistles that Father calls the flowers of Scotland. And her fingers have often roamed over the scrolls, coming together at the nameplate, elegant but forthright: 16 *Royal Terrace.* She feels the smooth, strong iron on her fingers, and then her fingers slowly feel the soft-ness of fur and also the roughness of a woollen blanket. And hears the woman asking for her name.

But no, no, it must not be spoken of! And Eveline is in danger of being pulled back behind the iron gates into the icy air, nearly slipping on the slippery path and being held up by Mother. *It is so cold, so frosty. Frosty.*

'Your name, miss?'

'Eveline. Eveline F – ' She cannot. She must not. But of course! 'Eveline Frost.'

'So be it, Eveline Frost. You are safe and warm and get-ting better. As is your babe. And what name have you given her?'

The infant is sleeping peacefully in the hamper, being the most convenient cradle for Meg to transport. She has carried it upstairs last thing of an evening, after banking the range and setting the bread to rise, then back down to the kitchen of a morning.

'Your little one, Miss Eveline?' Meg persists. She knows how to address someone who has arrived wearing fine garments, an expensive fur coat and soft kid gloves. Not to mention the charmingly foolish boots.

Evie experiences a wave of delight as she looks into the tiny face. She remembers such a wizened face when William was born. Funny, sweet little William, how we had such fun chasing about in the summer. And Jean and Izzie, and May. Oh, what can we do with May, who is so singular and I am sure will become a bluestocking and enrage Father. And Florence. Her dearest sister, but the horror and sobbing when this baby came pushing out. How did it happen? Why was it me? Where are they now? Where am I?

'Did you name the little one, Miss Eveline?'

'Name?' Evie can still only think dimly. 'Baby,' she replies.

'We cannot just call her Baby. What do you say that you call her a proper name for the while?'

Evie is fixated on the memory of her sister's face. 'F – F – Florence.'

'Florence it is then and it will be Florrie before long, that's for sure.'

Evie knows immediately that this is not right. Florence despises the name Florrie and could not abide Flo. 'No, not Florrie, never. And it mustn't be Flo. It must be – ' Her mind lurches over her friends and her mother and her siblings to her little brother. 'William.'

'Miss Eveline, William is not a proper name for a female child. Do you mean Wilhelmina and we might call her Minny?'

'Definitely not. Minny is our maid – that is – . But not William? Then must be Willy? Or maybe Billy? Billy, yes indeed!' Evie's mouth curls triumphantly.

Meg says nothing for a while, cogitating the obstinate yet naïve young lady. We must humour her, and it is not for me to name the little thing. Billy indeed. But wait – she has heard of Billie spelled in a feminine way. Yes, it is quite pretty.

'Then Billie it is for the time being, miss, if you're satisfied.' She smiles at mother and child.

Thus Billie Frost is so ordained.

Over the following days, Evie regains most of her mind and convalesces well. She never recalls her wild and feverish lurch along the northern terraces with a hamper, or the slippery weave down the rutty hill until her frozen feet gave way and she crumbled to the ground. But she recalls that she was to be sent away and her baby was to be given up. She knows she has scandalised and disgraced her family, and that she can never go back. She will not talk about her family, ever, even though her heart calls for them. She decides to put it out of her mind; stubborn as Father and determined as Mother. Yes, of course they must be spared her disgrace; they must not ever find her.

She shall now be Miss Eveline Frost, and she shall have such a grand time with baby Billie.

CHAPTER SEVEN

Meg and Alf think long and hard over the first weeks. They could have created a story about Eveline being a widow but she is obviously far too young to be married. They could have said she applied for a maid's position and was accepted but Meg knows this wouldn't wash amongst the locals – there is no denying the young lady's breeding. They know that mother and child might be still be claimed, but if not Meg and Alf must think about the future, especially how Eveline and Billie will be seen and treated in public.

And so, with agreement by Evie the announcement is made: that she is a young friend come to live here for the while, and a great help she will be too if she stays on. End of story; Meg is not one to be challenged on the whys or wherefores.

Alf's best mate, Sean O'Fee, generally known as Shuran, has a strong opinion on most things, and on this occasion he states, 'Sure an' nuttin' is new since Eve bit da apple. God bless ye in yer troubles.'

'Troubles be dashed,' replies Alf. 'This is a gift from Heaven above, and I'd thank you for leaving out the trouble.'

'Sure an' I didn't mean anyt'ing contrary, Alf, but surely ye have enough without such arseways complications? Oh, Alfie, don't take on so; I meant no harm in it. I can see ye dote on da child and da mammy too. An' dis little charmer willn't ever want for a better Da. Sure, even 'tis claimed and sent home – Jasus, Alfie, 'tis not what I meant to say a'tall! I was only sayin' – but I see ye're determined; sure an' you'll be grand, so.'

Meg's closest friend is Ernestine Struthers. She has come from Glasgow but is not of the Protestant persuasion. Nessie has many tales to tell in such a rapid, broad burr that Meg is lucky to catch half of her words, and the latest information is that a proper Catholic Church is soon to be built. 'Ye ken the first Mass was celebrated oop loft of Burke's Brewery halfway doon to Port Chalmers? Verra convenient for their suppin'! But the jarney was long and it was more convenient when Father started celebrations doon yon local skittle alley. Och, aye the noo, when we get a proper church,' cackles Nessie, 'the laddies will have to show more respect before skivin' off after Mass for their wee drop!'

But even Nessie, who found humour in many things, was sceptical of the new lodgers at first. 'Ye're tellin' me, Meggy, it's a lassie and her bastard? Foundlings? Och, ye're lookin' for trouble noo! Better to send them to the nuns or the workhouse with nae questions.' And she initially urged Meg to send the unfortunates on their way, because surely with Evie's fine clothes someone will find them and charge them with kidnapping, and before you know it, it will be gaol.

But with each day of the first week she softens like a sucked toffee, and is soon enamoured of the two newcomers, especially the tiny Billie. 'Och, aye, dinna fesh wee gurlie. An' Meggy dear, lang may ye' lum reek, for a bairn is a bonnie wee gift in the sight of God.' A tear drops quietly from Nessie's eye. She has never born a live child, only several dead souls.

Meg is grateful for her kindness; she knows support from friends and neighbours will be very handy. Not that she doesn't think that convents do the best job they can for such mites. Probably better than the workhouse – but who knows what goes on behind the doors of either? No life for anyone, if truth be told. And she and Alf see no sense in washing their hands of a young lady in an unfortunate situation when the pair have landed on them in their childless state. And for another thing, there are as yet few orphanages in the province – only further north where the French and Irish Catholics have established themselves. So it is settled.

The first few weeks are challenging but Meg ensures Alf goes about his daily scavenge with old Dolly, and only begs that he will bring back no more of the likes. She has coaxed Evie into suckling her baby and success develops with each new day. Meg knows that a wet nurse is next-to-best for a babe, but best indeed is its own mother, and with this mother now amongst the common people whose instinct is for nursing their own, all is proceeding well enough. Evie is sometimes still dazed about the entire outcome of her circumstance but her maternal instinct comes to the fore and she is in constant attendance of baby Billie. She comes to know that her infant is not a doll that she can pick up and put down and play with at will; she also learns that broken nights and fractious days take a toll on one, even if one is fifteen and spirited.

Most importantly, she understands the constant fear of infant mortality – death that can come like a thief in the night, robbing without impunity. But Billie seems as determined as her own mother, and within weeks her bright eyes are fixing intensely on objects and movements. The stare that will become the Look.

Eveline does not, or will not, reveal anything of her identity, and her wish for silence is respected. Alf and Meg do what they decide honest people would do, and they place a notice in the newspaper.

> *FOUND: Young Lady with Baby, possibly lost memory. Apply Otago Witness Box 28.*

This does not bring forth any interest, and they agree there must be some other sort of enticement. Alf places the next notice two weeks later:

> *FROST: Young educated Lady seeks Family. Confidentiality assured. Apply Otago Witness Box 28.*

What a to-do this results in, with twelve applicants pleading varying agendas. There are those who have sniffed a chance and believe they could take a Lady into their care for a small sum. There are others who offer courtship, no doubt hopeful of a dowry – and what a dowry it would be, Meg laughs.

Mostly there are those who have lost their governess or maid to marriage and are looking for a replacement. Servants and their lack of suitability is a very common conundrum in the colony. Emigrant families may bring their maids, but what single woman can snub the chance of marriage and advancement? Some have come under the guise of a 'suitable woman' but are often mediocre at best and useless at worst and the overwhelming ratio of female to male is superb. This predicament often forces the more well-off to endure the inconvenience of advertising for servants.

No one applies to advise that they have lost a daughter.

Alf writes back to each of them as dictated by Meg, advising that their application is unsuccessful. 'I think, Alfie,' she says, 'we must think of something better. I know, we don't want to be in the position of losing the little pigeons, but if we are challenged sometime down the road – say someone thought we had done a kidnap or similar! – we could be in trouble. I think we must put it more particular, so as to try and reunite the family. And then we can say we've done our best.'

The next and final advertisement is straight to the point:

REWARD: Young educated Woman and Baby seek to reunite with Frost family. Apply Otago Witness Box 28.

This time three replies are received, each forcefully claiming to be the very Frosts. Alf replies to them as before and arranges to meet each applicant. Of course it must be away from Maclaggan Street, and it is decided to conduct these encounters in the private lounge of the new Queens Arms Hotel, south on Princes Street.

The first couple look strained and tired, arriving by bullock cart from west of Outram. Their daughter has run away from home and they have no idea where, but have heard she may be in trouble. If it is the trouble, there is nowt to fret on as they shall provide for them with great certainty.

'And what does she look like, if you please?' asks Alf.

'She is a strapping lass, the eldest of seven, only three alive now, and we had such hopes for her future in New Zealand. She's like her mother here, brown eyes, and curling black hair. Look, here is a likeness – not very good, but you will see her strong looks.'

Nothing like Eveline's. Alf's heart goes out to them, but knows they are not the ones. The woman clutches her husband as they stand up to leave, and murmurs, 'Any road, if you do come upon our girl, please, oh please let us know directly.'

And so goes a family in tatters after the disappearance of their daughter. Who is to know if she has drowned in a river, or got lost in the hills, or run away in shame?

The following day a second pair of claimants sweep into the Queen's Arms lounge, looking about as if they expect to see a young woman and a baby with the gentleman agent. They are nothing like the first Frosts. Well-heeled but too clever by half, thinks Alf after the first two minutes, merely allowing them to create their own scenario. Oh, they are ever so pleased their girl has been found, everyone is frantic with worry as the wicked thing has stolen her aunt's baby.

'Or that is how it seemed after she was gone, because no, of course she is not wicked, and must have just fallen and lost her senses! After all that education, just to think of it! But whatever the reason, she is welcome back with us immediately. We will obviously be doing you a significant favour, sir, in taking her, that is claiming her – and of course the baby. And what, may I ask, is the reward you are offering?'

That evening Alf has great pleasure in miming the antics of the second Mr and Mrs Frost, reducing Meg to stitches. 'Yes, indeed, probably would call himself the Duke of York if the occasion warranted it. Him and his lady friend carrying on like that, just thinking about the reward. Deary me, only one more lot to go then.'

But the third applicant does not arrive for the interview. The Maguires have done their best. No authentic claimants by the name of Frost, and so now what?

They continue to put much thought into the situation over the following weeks. That is, Meg discusses it with Alf, who agrees with most things in the fullness of time, after a firm defence of the odds to ensure his soft nature is not taken advantage of. Such discussions usually end with 'Well, my darlin', if that is what you think is best, we shall agree that it shall be done.'

And the agreement is that they keep these orphans of circumstance under their own roof until she is properly claimed or – more hopefully – until the seas run dry. For Meg and Alf have formed an attachment so strong that it would break their hearts to see their charges leave. They know that one day it may come to pass, and to guard the accuracy of their own story they keep copies of the advertisements, and Alf's subsequent notes. Meg is torn between emotions, the stronger being that she feels Evie is like a much younger sister, and treats her with love and care. Alf adores her too, and Billie is like the child they never had. Already she is wrapped around his heart like a tender vine. Life is hard, but plenty of cheer abounds in the slums. And so Billie Frost survives the perils of infancy amongst the common folk of Maclaggan Street.

Eveline is a most welcome hand in Meg's kitchen, even though she is all fingers and thumbs at first. She is lively and willing to help where she can. She has her daily tasks and before long is indispensable. Throngs of new arrivals need their victuals and plenty is provided, with Meg's astute ways of giving what always seems more for their money – pearl barley soup to fill, mutton stew for vitality, an abundance of fresh silver beet for the bowels – whilst making a steady profit herself.

Although Maguires operates without dispensing liquor, many merry times are to be had of an evening. Evie has never regained memory of how she arrived, but has built confidence over the past two years to sing like she did before at – but no, not that – and is happy to trill her sweet voice after supper. She has blossomed from a bewildered girl into a poised young woman. She receives *bravos* from the parlour's guests and there is often a moist eye during recitals.

Billie's sleep patterns leave her wide awake until late evening, so it is accepted that she stays with the adults rather than in her bed alone upstairs. She toddles amongst the guests and rides on their knees. She leans on Evie as she sings, and warbles her own versions. She follows Meg as the last cups of tea are offered, and carefully proffers the cake plate. Billie is much cosseted and indulged, but remains without guile. Yet there is something wise and old about the child, and although she is generally biddable, at times a violet spark of indignation flames across her sloping golden eyes. She often refuses assistance, whether getting in a tangle putting on her dress or buttoning her shoes, stating clearly, 'I do mine-ownself.'

'Well I never,' is all Meg can say to this increasing independence.

While three humans watch over Billie, Mungo is her true guardian. His place at Maguires is never questioned; he is the humble servant who will lay down his doggy life for her. Blind in one eye and with a mangled ear, Mungo is always on guard. In the evenings he shadows Billie vigilantly as she offers around the sultana cake.

'Not two,' Billie admonishes a surprised gentleman who reaches again towards the platter.

'But I believe you are now two! It is said that you are two years old and a clever girl,' is the response.

Billie's spun-toffee hair flicks from side to side and her

eyes are indignant. 'Not two cake,' she instructs. 'Not one-two-free-four-fi-sic-seben. You take only *one* cake!'

CHAPTER EIGHT

─────〜〜〜─────

January 1862

The town is in an uproar. Gold was discovered last year in a bleak gully near Dunstan, some two hundred miles inland, and vast wealth is predicted. The *Otago Witness* has declared boldly: 'Gold, Gold, Gold, is the universal subject of conversation. The gold fever is running to such a height that, if it continues, there will be scarcely a man left in town.'

The Maguires continue to earn a steady living by their shrewd but kind-hearted hospitality in the rapidly expanding slums. A steady flow of humanity arrives at Port Chalmers. Some survive the journey physically but not so well in mind, having lost babies, children, husbands or wives during an appalling journey. Others are keenly focused on making a new life on the land. The rest are desperate to embark on the next stage of their great expectations along the Dunstan trail. Most of these fling their swags over their shoulders and trudge up the narrow dirt track to Dunedin before heading for the diggings where it is said that the rivers spew forth gold nuggets. Some stay and get thoroughly drunk before the journey and by nightfall their tents are dotted all over the hillside. Others, although they too see gold and fortune, have the coin for a night of civilised comfort, and Maguire's Private Hotel offers wholesome board plus eight beds sardined into the upstairs rooms. Many guests are single males, but some are couples or families that have transferred from one form of poverty into another by way of eternal hope. Meg cannot host these guests without being paid, but she will occasionally give a penniless newcomer a mattress for the night before gently but firmly asking them to move on. And there are some who try to take advantage, moving on and coming back, hoping for another two days before the next bullock train, but she stands firm as others arrive with their meagre possessions. The stream is steady and unrelenting.

According to the superior-thinking Scots, the immigrants pouring into Dunedin are 'the new iniquity', diluting their vision of godly perfection. Meg and Alf do not choose to be affronted and they continue to keep an honest board and bed for their continuous flow of guests. Not all new arrivals are bent on booze and bawdiness, gravitating to the public houses before wildly pressing on over hill and plain to the perceived riches of the diggings. Most are steadfast, happy to pay the going rate of two shillings per night for a few days of plain wholesomeness, and Maguires is a palace compared to their narrow, lurching bunks aboard ship. Plus there is literally music to their ears every evening except Sunday, from 'the lovely Miss Eveline' who sings in the small parlour. She has taken to wearing a thin golden band for convenience and discretion, and is also assumed to be young Mrs Frost. The nightly event has become quite an occasion, often orchestrated by three-year-old Billie:

'First with "Jenny's Petticoat", Mama.'

'Yes, wee girl, and it's called "Comin' Thro' the Rye",'

'You told me Comin' not correct, Mama, it should be Coming.'

'Only in this instance it is a song, already with the words established, Billie. Now please let me start the recital.'

'Stablished. Good words when stablished, Mama. Now you begin!'

Evie draws breath, smiles around the room and duly begins:

> 'Oh, Jenny's wet, poor body,
> Jenny's seldom dry,
> She dragged all her petticoats
> Comin' thro' the rye!'

The guests join in each chorus, quietly at first, some dabbing at the corner of their eyes.

> If a body meet a body
> Comin' thro' the rye,
> If a body kiss a body

Need a body cry?
'Ev'ry lassie has her laddie
None, I say, have I,
Yet all the laddies smile at me
When comin' thro' the rye!

Occasionally a bold young man will venture comments such as 'And no wonder they smile at you, miss, if you pardon me saying so!'

The smiles and quiet bravos tell their own story, and rarely does anyone frown like Father at the notion of kissing. That is the part where the sadness of her early life, and the wrench from Mother and Father and her siblings, clutches at Evie's throat, but she takes a deep breath and continues. 'Skye Boat Song' is next, after which she asks for requests, and they come quickly: 'Purple Heather' and 'Scarborough Fair'; 'Highland Mary' and 'Ye Banks and Braes'; then, 'Dawning of the Day' and 'The Wind that Shakes the Barley'.

And more learned from guests who wish something to be sung or, on occasions, are happy to take a turn. Most guests hail from England, Scotland and Ireland, and those from Australia have mostly originated from the same parts. The Australians are not of those who were depopulated from England and Ireland for petty crimes or political leanings. They are mainly those who sailed originally for New South Wales or Victoria of their free will. Their songs of choice are 'The Wild Colonial Boy' in which the men's voices often chorus the rebellious words, and 'She Moved through the Fair' requested by the women. Evie knows it brings on the tears with its mordant melody, and she will only sing the first two verses and reprise the first.

My young love said to me,
My mother won't mind
And my father won't slight you
For your lack of kind.
And she stepped away from me
And this she did say:
It will not be long, love,
Till our wedding day.
She stepped away from me
And she moved through the fair
And fondly I watched her
Move here and move there.
And then she made her way homeward,
With one star awake,
As the swan in the evening
Moved over the lake.
My young love said to me,
My mother won't mind
And my father won't slight you
For your lack of kind.
And she stepped away from me
And this she did say:

It will not be long, Love
Till our wedding day.

Tears flow as predicted, but then it is quickly on to more buoyant tunes such as the rollicking 'Clementine' (oh, how many songs are about disaster – fell into the foaming brine indeed!) and 'Cherry Ripe' (where everyone is happy, thankfully!) to retrieve the positive mood. Evie does not sing coarse or vulgar songs, partly because Billie is always present even when she falls asleep in Alf's arms, and partly because just up the street there are plenty of bawdy houses where the tempo is raucous.

The final song is always 'The Gypsy Girl's Dream' and the notion of dwelling in marble halls falls softly over the sleepy audience. Evie sings with sweet grace and as they head towards their rest, the guests often whisper 'Pretty indeed' and 'Most pleasurable.'

'Pleasurable,' murmurs Billie in her half-sleep as she is gathered up in her mother's arms and carried up the steep stairs to their shared bed.

CHAPTER NINE

By the end of the year, fourteen more hotels have sprung up in and around Maclaggan Street. Even so, Maguires is almost always a full house with little time for conversation. To compensate, Meg and Eveline sometimes spend their evenings beside the kitchen fire, stitching and chatting. It is a companionable time.

'Stuff and nonsense,' says Meg firmly. This night they are talking about the sorry state of a neighbour whose devotion to the bottle is the cause of much misery to his wife and eight living children. Their abode is a wooden shack, built some ten years ago around the same time that the Maguires erected their little palace, but now ramshackle with a leaking roof and broken windows. The woman of the house sleeps on the floor and the children share two rank mattresses. A dire situation, only too common around Maclaggan Street.

'It's unacceptable in my book. No excuses. If you don't have work, you go and find it. If a man can't provide for his family despite whatever the good Lord has sent his way – begging your pardon, Lord – then the man has no testicular fortitude. If the demon drink has him in its sights and the man can't look it in the eye and say 'Be gone, Satan!' then that pitiful man has not got what made him into a man in the first place. No spine. No testicular fortitude.'

Meg and Evie often discuss the high and the mighty; the elevated and the lowered; and the popular topic of men – especially the man who has fallen into the path of all evil through a weak will or any excuse for bad behaviour. But they also bring themselves up short with a sigh when the conversation throws a slant on men and their ways, and the ways that brought Evie to the street.

'What is test – test-ular fortitude?'

A small voice, without guile or any other motive than a child overhearing adult conversation, stops them short this time. Billie is in her curled-up place under the kitchen table. 'What is test-ular fortitude, Mama?'

'All shirt and no trousers,' states Meg, then claps her hand over her mouth, realising that the child's ears have been flapping.

Evie takes up the response: 'It – it means having gumption, being brave, and doing the right thing even if you are scared. But it's time you were up in bed.'

'Then I must have test-ular fortitude, Mama.'

'No, Billie, indeed that is not what you have!'

Billie's eyebrows knit, knowing that what Mama says should be obeyed. But with a wisdom far beyond her three years she cannot be content. She cringes as she thinks of the privy down the back garden. Mother Meg calls it a dunny, but Mama corrects Billie to the more refined word. Whatever its name, nothing terrifies her more than that infinite black hole with its rotten-egg stench of lime sulphur. The only thing that allows her to manage the ordeal without crying out, is the thought of her little companion Mungo waiting by the door. It is as if he senses the need for distraction from her torment, and is ready for race-me as soon as Billie flings herself free.

'But, Mama, when I go out to the dunny – um, the privy, I must be brave. I'm not afraid of the dark, and I'm not afraid of the spiders, not very much. But I am afraid of – of when I get up on the seat, of slipping right through, falling all the way through to China. And I am so, so afraid. But, Mama, I think of Mungo waiting for me by the door, and am brave and strong and quickly jump down and I am safe. So why, Mama? Why if I am being brave and strong why cannot I have test-ular fortitude?'

Meg and Evie eye each other helplessly. They know Mungo waits for her out there. He is such a comical dog, with stumpy legs, a long body, and a shaggy head that doesn't seem to fit; as if he was put together in a hurry with no time to check the parts. One ear cocks forward and one back, and even his black patches are of a peculiar placement. But Mungo is a very smart dog, and they are glad Billie has such a constant companion.

'Heavens!' breathes Evie. 'I beg your pardon, I'm sure. I didn't know you were so very afraid of that old privy. So you indeed have fortitude. But not test – you are a girl and so you just have – have – fortitude.'

'Fortitude,' muses Billie and squeezes her eyes tight against the terror of that black hole. And so she learns that to be brave has a handsome new name.

CHAPTER TEN

Alf treasures his reading time allocated for three o'clock each afternoon, sometimes sitting in the warmth of his kitchen alcove or, if it should be sunny, in the front window of what might grandly be called the parlour. He reads his weekly *Witness* and its daily rival voraciously, and he is always thankful that he learned to read back Home, a rare thing for a boy of his background. His mentor was his uncle, who put a great store in book learning, and Alf is determined that his Billie shall have the same.

Not that Billie needs to be coerced; she snuggles up to him most days and seems to absorb information like a thirsty throat. She is permitted only to speak at certain intervals, otherwise Alf does not get his peace, and from five minutes to four, she watches the mantel clock for the eternal minutes to pass before the o'clock. At this time she may pick a headline or advertisement and ask Alf to read them aloud. She then repeats them herself, word for word:

DUNEDIN FLOUR AND BARLEY MILLS. Fine flour, best quality and Pot Barley. Highest prices given for Wheat and Barley. Oats bruised and Hay Chaffed on reasonable terms.

HORSES, HORSES, HORSES. Twenty saddle & harness horses on sale at Goodall's Paddock, Tokomariro. Can be bought privately off Mr Goodall, or T. Miles, Importer.

More recently, full paragraphs are what she requests, even if some are thinly disguised as news:

A PUBLIC MEETING will be held on the Evening of FRIDAY, the 5th of April, at half past Seven o'clock p.m., in the Provincial Hotel, Stafford Street, to take into consideration the best method of testifying to A. J. BURNS Esq., the high esteem in which he is held by the working classes of this community, for the successful efforts displayed by him in maintaining the Eight-Hours System of Labour at the Settlement of this Province.

'Fancy that, my love.' Even tedious reports that are of limited interest to Alf do not appear to deter Billie and she races on:

A letter was read from Hayman Joseph, of the Hebrew persuasion, applying for the Town Board office on Sunday next and succeeding Sabbath, for the use of his co-religionists. The clerk was authorised to express the regret of the Board at their inability to accede to the application.

'What is the Hebrew persuasion, Alf? And what is co-religionists?' She is curious about all things and always gravely ponders Alf's explanations before proceeding.

DUNEDIN, OTAGO, NEW ZEALAND. Designs and Drawings for a new Gaol at Highcliff will be received at the Office of the Provincial Secretary, until 4 p.m., the second day of March, 1863. The following Premiums will be given to the successful competitors, viz:–

For the Gaol, 1st Prize, £150, 2nd Prize, £75.

For the Hospital, 1st prize, £100, 2nd prize, £50.

For the Lunatic Asylum, 1st prize, £100, 2nd Prize, £50.

'Oh, Alf, how amusing it would be to design a Gaol! Now the next, please, Alfie.'

'Amusing, I'm sure. Very well, and this will be the last for today, my love,' smiles Alf and Billie is already tracing the page to find the longest block of words. She reads on, far ahead of her four years, stumbling from time to time and stopping to ask Alf the meaning of new words. Meg has said, 'You'll be a fool unto yourself, Alfie, spoiling that child,' but Alf is not dissuaded. Billie reads doggedly on:

THE GOLD FIELDS MANUAL FOR NEW ARRIVALS. We publish the following information concerning the gold fields for the benefit of new arrivals:– The principal gold fields of Otago are those at Tuapeka, Waitahuna, Waipori, Woolshed Creek, Mount Highlay, Dunstan and Nokomai Diggings, and several minor fields, such as Coal Creek, Lindis, the Dunstan River, Shag River, and Moeraki Beach. Tuapeka, although not the oldest, is the best known and most extensively worked gold field Gabriel's Gully, the scene of Mr. Read's early discoveries.

'That is enough, my love, you have done well, but enough today,' sighs Alf indulgently.

'But, Alf – oh, Alf, how I adore your soft whiskers – but, Alf, there is still more inside the lines,' Billie persists.

'It isn't like you to try flattery, miss. Yes, there is more inside the border; you have been crafty with your choice. But it is four-thirty on the clock, and you must help lock up the chooks and do your other jobs before you lay the table.'

'Please, lovely Alf, just one more teeny-weeny bit?'

'Billie Frost, hear me now: if you whine there will be no more reading tomorrow. But I shall agree for you to read one more paragraph.'

She searches quickly:

There are about 4,000 miners on the Dunstan field. These appear to have done well. Six thousand ounces have been brought down by escort, 2,000 ounces have reached town by private hand, and it is estimated that an equal quantity has been sent to Tuapeka, making an aggregate of 10,000 ounces. Large quantities still remain in the hands of the miners owing to the want of cash on the field for purchasing. A fortnightly escort service has now been established.

'Escort service, Alf, that's for catching robbers! Do you – '

But Alf has closed the *Witness* with a deep inhalation of breath, and that is enough for Billie to slide off his knee and make haste out of the parlour with a backwards tilt of her head.

Alf grins like a fool. Great Scott, she seems to absorb information through her stubby finger, and her memory is infinite. Rarely can he fault her comprehension once the words are explained. At the age of four, when most children are yet illiterate – and many of this district will always will be so – Billie is reading to the level of a well-educated ten-year-old. Alf shakes his head as he returns to his paper before the light from the parlour window.

CHAPTER ELEVEN

———～～———

August 1863

Eveline takes an unwilling Billie to town. The child wishes to stay and play with Mungo, but she needs proper shoes for next week's excursion to Port Chalmers, and not just hand-me-downs this time.

Although her family disowned her – or in effect she has rejected them – she will not disown herself or her precious daughter. She is now a reasonably accomplished seamstress and not only is their attire always smart, but she now earns a fee for small orders. She attends enough clients to keep her very busy, some of whom gift her any remnants, which she delicately incorporates into her slim, but fashionable, wardrobe. Only last week she was able to add a corded embellishment to her best hat.

She walks purposefully down the rutted hill, along the Rattray Street slope and into the dirt road grandly named

Princes Street. She wears a deep-brown bombardine skirt flat-pleated into a narrow waist, chestnut velveteen jacket and a cream lace jabot. The neat hat of interwoven moiré and velveteen, with its new silken twist cocking up the side, is as fine as any lady's. The paisley shawl of heathery purples and browns is wrapped tightly around her shoulders; it is still a week away from spring and still very raw.

Billie wears a stout grey tweed coat cut down from one of Meg's that is now too tight; she has stitched it with love and humour upon instructions from Billie as to its style – 'opening so the under shows out.'

'That will never keep your chest warm, my love,' she tuts. To compensate, what shows out is a high-necked bodice of violet gabardine which, with a matching tam-o'shanter, brings out the indescribable colour of her eyes.

They turn into the Princes Street cutting and soon pass the handsome Farley's Buildings – stone and brick, and unlike any of its wooden neighbours – which houses ground-floor shops, upstairs offices, a meeting hall and a photography studio. They pass Collins the fruiterer, McLeod & Gibson the grocers, Ure & Co with its large chests of tea, and Bray's the hatter, before arriving at their destination. The Golden Boot is operated by the Walsh brothers who strive for elegance as well as practicality. Billie is still out of sorts but when they enter the Ladies' Sitting Room with its array of fine leathers, kids, and fabrics – all totally unsuited to the muddy streets – she instantly becomes fascinated.

Evie selects two samples. Strong black ankle boots with

thick leather laces, practical but smart. Then a handsome oxblood, high-buttoned style that will have room to grow when the toes are stuffed with newspaper.

'Mama, may I try on these wee white ones, most gorgeous and shiny, and oh, look at their dear little heels and the many glass buttons. Two, four, eight times two equals sixteen buttons, Mama!' Billie is thrilled with the delicate style.

Mr Damian Walsh who reigns over the shop looks stunned at such quick calculations.

'Of course not, they will never be suitable for – that is, you may not need – ' Evie does not wish to give away her circumstances.

'Oh, Mama, please just one little time, just for the pleasurable?'

'It's "pleasure" in this instance, Billie, but no, you shall not try them on today. Let's try these oxblood ones, if you please, Mr Walsh.' Billie's affections then transfer to the shiny deep-red boots and their groupings of buttons, and she is satisfied.

'I do believe we shall take them in two sizes larger; this way extra stockings shall keep her feet very warm,' she says firmly. It is true that warm stockings are always a necessity in Dunedin's chilling winter.

Mr Damian enjoys the talking, the gossiping and the wooing of customers. Several of them treat him as a confidant, and he is privy to a range of information. He knows what two sizes larger means – they must last two years. 'You will be pleased with these, I'm sure, madam. And,' he coughs slightly, 'if they're regularly polished they will keep well.'

If it wasn't for his genuine charm he could be rather oily, thinks Evie as he goes on with his pitch.

'I hope you would pardon me, madam, but I must say both your coat – that is yours and your daughter's – are most elegant. Your seamstress is obviously very well trained and with an excellent eye for detail. And the stitching is so perfect. What quality, what style, and what a grand costume the young miss has too. Here you are then,' as he presents the wrapped boots, 'and that will be one pound, thank you, madam.'

'Gracious, a pound for a child's boots?' Evie had suspected these shoes might be more than the eight shillings she'd planned on spending – but twenty shillings?

'These ones are imported, madam, and there is a shilling tax on them.'

'A shilling extra for tax! Oh, I beg your pardon, Mr Walsh, but we must change –'

'Yes, two years ago they would have only been nineteen shillings,' he says with regret.

'Nineteen shillings!' repeats Evie, feeling faint.

Mr Damian is enamoured, and keen to be as kind as possible. 'Bless me, I'm forgetting! We're moving further up the Cutting next week, madam, and we are giving a discount on certain goods at the minute. So these boots are only fourteen shillings and sixpence.

Evie looks into her purse and decides that she shall pay

this amount for the privilege of knowing she has chosen well.

The proprietor assesses her hesitation and makes another assumption, then says, 'But just one moment, madam, I think my brother Mr Joseph is calling me.'

He steps nimbly out to the stockroom and returns beaming. 'So glad I am that I heard my brother call out! He reminded me that these little beauties are the last ones, and so they are to be sold for ten shillings and six pence. A marvellous purchase!'

Evie completes the sale with a smile of gratitude that sends Mr Damian Walsh's pulse racing. Billie gazes at the white kid slippers again, but is satisfied with her high-buttoned boots. She will not call the colour oxblood and searches for a more suitable name. 'Mother Meg's sideboard – this is most like it,' she declares. The piece of furniture that has been in Meg's family for generations and was shipped out from Home a few years back is a deep, rich mahogany, polished with love and gleaming. Billie's new boots are therefore mahogany.

'They're cracker, my love,' states Alf.

'Mahogany boots. Cracker and marvellous,' she agrees.

CHAPTER TWELVE

Alf, Evie and Billie board a barge bound for Port Chalmers. It will take only thirty minutes to the end of Otago Harbour, and they will be transported to a world of ships arriving and departing. They are on their way to welcome Alf's two brothers and their families who have decided, like himself many years ago, to strike out for a new land. Alf has decided that the journey by bullock and cart around the hillside is far too torturous, and that it is worth the sum of half a penny each way to take the lighter from Dunedin to the port. They shall then return in style on the paddle steamer *Golden Age*.

The southern peninsula protects Dunedin town from the ocean, and trees grow from the summit of the hills to the very water's edge, forming a continuous panorama of wild beauty. They chug past the hamlets around Portobello on the southern coast and St Leonards on the northern, marvelling at the abundant birdlife darting about and the marine mammals splayed casually on the rocks, and keeping

a lookout for dolphins. It was Billie's fifth birthday yesterday, and as usual her mind is racing.

'Stop fidgeting, Billie!' Evie is somewhat cross because
her best boots pinch across the toes. 'If you fall overboard
then there you'll be, in the water and me unable to swim to
your rescue.'

Billie's eyes enlarge with the thought of the deep indigo
sea engulfing her, before she laughs. 'Mama, you are ever so
funny! You know I shall not fall in, and even if I should,
Alf will toss me a rope.' Such is her confidence from having
been both cosseted and let go her own way – not for her the
thought of tumbling over like a baby.

Alf and Evie exchange looks and then make silent
prayers, as do many plying this journey when passing
Sawyer's Bay. Not three months before, *Pride of the Yarra*
carrying fifty passengers for Dunedin had been run down
by the paddle boat *Favorite* steaming outwards to Port
Chalmers, catching her from the bow and staving her plates
almost to the starboard side. She went down with thirteen
souls lost in the cold, choking water. The entire province
still seems to be talking about how it could possibly have
happened on an early evening with unremarkable weather
or light.

Port Chalmers is calamitous, with twenty-seven vessels
in port and nine more to be towed up from the Heads this
day, including the *Crimea* on which Alf's family have made
their passage. Following one day behind is the splendid, new
City of Dunedin carrying three hundred souls and Alf's family were keen to make their passage on her maiden voyage.

But she sailed from Glasgow over three hundred miles north of London and sense won out over sensibility. So the *Crimea* it was to be, and after eighty-six days at sea they will be amongst the hundred passengers soon arriving at their destination.

The moody, ever-changing current of the outer harbour slaps at the jetties. Sailing ships with their massive sails furled, brigs, barques, schooners, paddle steamers, clippers – it is busier than they could have imagined, even though they are aware that over three hundred vessels have entered the harbour so far this year. Some carry dry goods, building supplies, cattle and sheep. Some bring full contingents of emigrants. Yet other ships bring thousands upon thousands of prospectors bound for the gold fields of Central Otago.

Buildings along the wharf sport bunting and decorations from the recent annual regatta; public demonstrations of rejoicing are a regular thing at Port Chalmers town. The docks and streets are seething with disembarking families, unsteady from three months at sea. Relatives and friends are cheering and welcoming. Sailors are carousing while deserters and feckless gold seekers are taking to the hills. Pedlars, pimps, prostitutes, local citizens and merchants go about their daily toil. Hotels pump out beer and measures of whisky and the more genteel establishments also offer wine and cake. 'Money runs like water in Port Chalmers!' mimic the diggers, and their own uproarious antics flow likewise.

'Keep close, Billie. It is very crowded and I don't want to lose you while we wait. I believe we have nearly an hour before they will disembark, and then we shall all go to an hotel for a pot of tea and cake.'

Although she is used to people coming and going, Billie has never seen so many at one time, even in Dunedin town.

There are people who look like themselves: colonials. Sturdy children looking healthy against the new chums' white, pinched faces. Perhaps it is the sun that shows them up in a different light or perhaps it is the skin of the people who look sun-kissed. Mama says to be sun-kissed is acceptable but to be sun-browned is not, and in summer she must wear her bonnet. But today is the first day of spring, still very crisp, and the sun is weak and not in a kissing humour.

But to those disembarking after four months at sea, all is light and bright. There are families looking pale and unbalanced. There are men with crumpled shirts and trousers, wide hats, and swags on their back.

There are elegant gentlemen and stylish ladies promenading or sitting in groups, children breaking away to play, and others moving briskly about and blowing into their hands. Steam is coming from Billie's mouth too, and she catches it and releases its spent form into the salt air.

She is entranced with other ladies, the kind she does not see in Maclaggan Street; Mother says that fine ladies live up The Rise. Although Mother's dresses are beautiful, with some lace or satin or feathers when she is going out, but some of these ladies' costumes are very fine indeed, even though some of their shoes are ridiculous for the mud and she sees more than one catch their little heels between the dock boards. Billie sees a lot of shoes, and counts up to fifty, then counts up to fifty again. 'Now I shall look at the skirts,' she tells herself, and watches all styles of practical and fine getups, some with their rear projections dipping onto the boards. Black, grey, mauve, olive, ecru, plus stronger flashes of colour in capes, shawls, bonnets and gloves. From watching her mother's inventive cutting and sewing, and from collecting the scraps, Billie has come to know the difference between moiré, bombazine, tartan, tweed and velvet. And then there are bustles, pleats, swags, biases and braids that are fashionable daytime wear for ladies. She is not tall enough to calculate the array of mantles and paletots, gloves and hats, but at five years old Billie knows what's what about proper attire, and pats her own jacket and tam o'shanter.

In doing so, her eyes lift upwards, beyond the realm of skirts. People still mill about, the sky is brightly pale, but Mother is not there.

'Mama? Mama? Where are you? Alf, where have you gone?'

Billie stands tall now: the world is swirling around her; she is giddy from jumping up and from a sudden fright. 'Mama, where are you, naughty Mama!' and Billie feels annoyed.

But it is only momentary and she sees what she must do. Find Mama. And singing always helps, says Mama, so Billie starts up quietly, off key as usual:

Speed, bonnie boat, like a bird on the wing,
Onward! The sailors cry;

Carry the lad that's born to be king
Over the sea to Skye.
Loud the winds howl, loud the winds roar,
Thunderclaps rend the air –

She usually shouts that second evocative stanza, but now it starts to unsettle her. She will not sing, just hum. Billie starts along the wharf, looking this way and that. Past ships with their disembarking passengers and their embracing relatives. Past the pedlars and painted ladies, past the profusion of ship chandlers, sailmakers and provedors, until she arrives at an open space. Her world once again whirls about her head and she is almost overcome by the crowds that pour to and from the pentagon of roads. Again she cries in bewilderment, 'Mama! Mama!'

When the feeling subsides she decides that Mama must have gone on towards the place where a pot of tea and possibly cake will be waiting, and she makes her way across to the Custom House and the National Bank, to the town's main sloped road. George Street is lined with a variety of grocers and merchants, hotels and saloons, and tearooms, all busy with trade. The brisk spring afternoon does not daunt people from sitting at outside tables, taking tea and cake, ale and stronger stuff.

At each interval Billie stops and asks, politely as she has been taught: 'Excuse me, may I speak? Have you seen my mama, Mrs Frost? She will be looking for me.'

Some folk reply to the contrary and some ignore her, immersed in their own business. Some are concerned and ask, 'Are you lost, wee girl?' to which Billie responds, 'Not at all; only my mother has lost me.' Others dismiss her as a potential pickpocket and clutch their purses tight.

But Billie plods determinedly up the stony hill, inspecting the interior of the First Bank of Otago, and the first of many hotels. She peers into Wilson's butchery with its live fowls in baskets and severed pig heads that squint their dead eyes at her; Kettle's grocery store with its sacks of wheat, corn and coffee; on and on until the buildings dwindle. She stops and gazes back down towards the port, where the distant ships' masts seem to weave a cat's cradle of lines, blurring her determination. But she must cross to the other side of the road to the Apothecaries Hall and start her task downhill. Past the stables, past the ship chandler, past the fishmonger. At each point of reference Billie addresses the same question to the milling crowds: 'Excuse me, have you seen my mama, Mrs Frost? She is wearing a fine purple shawl.'

She stares into the window of Reuben Tom's apothecary with its rows of deeply coloured bottles. At Ritchie's Bakery she is immersed in the warm yeasty aromas, but doesn't waste time at the fish shop. Her voice is quavering now, even though singing is trying to make it better. 'Singing cockles and mussels alive, alive-o ... sweet Molly Malone, singing ... '

At a table just inside the doorway of the Provincial Hotel, an elegant gentleman is sipping whisky with his companions. Like the greater contingent of visitors, he is also waiting for arriving passengers. A small girl apologises for knocking against him. He glances up. A surge of prickly chills – a ghost walking over his grave – rushes over his body. He is disturbed. There is something about the child's slanted eyes that momentarily catches his attention. It is as if – so similar to – but no, how absurd. He stares after her as she whirls her skirts and departs. He returns to his conversations.

Billie is weary now, but completes the full circuit and arrives at the apex where the five rutty roads converge. And there, by the entry to the wharf, is Mama! A small crowd is fussing around her and a policeman is taking notes. She is sobbing and being comforted by unknown people and there is a quite a commotion.

A shriek pierces the sea air. With relief, Evie turns to find a furious, red-faced girl hurtling towards her across the intersection. Oblivious of the horses, carts, billboards and throngs of people, the child hurtles through the convergence and flings herself on her mother. But only for a few seconds, then she tears herself off and stiffens into a rigid pose.

'You lost me!' Billie cries, her now-white face tipped accusingly, eyes blazing with tears that refuse to fall. 'You lost me, Mama, you lost me!'

'Hush, child, be done!' responds Evie as she clings to

her. 'I didn't lose you, you lost us! Gracious me, whatever next?'

'You did so too.' This time the voice has more control, but the Look remains.

'Billie Frost, do not take that disagreeable tone with me. I've been in such a frenzy this past hour. You must have been day-dreaming, for I was always here, and then – then I turned and you were gone. Darling one, thank the Lord that you are safe and sound! I persuaded dear Alf to go on to The George with his arrivals to take afternoon tea, since they are so weary. And we shall follow. But Billie, I didn't lose you, wee girl!' She clutches at the child's stiff form to draw her close.

Billie will not be comforted and her eyes glitter with furious love.

'Come on.' Evie takes Billie's arm so they can cross safely and walk up to the hotel – she is gasping for a long cup of tea after all the commotion. Then it will be back to Dunedin on the lighter, where the beds are ready and waiting for Alf's family.

But Billie is not consoled. She turns her head up at her mother, eyes now like steel.

'You. Lost. Me.' is the verdict.

CHAPTER THIRTEEN

⁓

March 1864

South District School welcomes Billie on its opening day. Known as Park's School after its well-loved headmaster, it is the first public school in Dunedin. Maclaggan Street children do not generally aspire to school, and in many cases the adults are vague about the number of children they have reared. Certainly most children would not be able to bring the penny required for a writing slate. But thanks to her Scots heritage, Evie believes education is of prime importance.

The Maguires are happy to support Evie's wishes and to encourage her education far beyond their own experiences. And although Evie always had a governess – allowing herself wisps of memory – she sees public school as modern and bold, and has saved hard to ensure her child starts as soon as possible. Most will start at age six, but she has met with Mr

Park to put her case and Billie has been granted a place some six months earlier.

From the first day, Billie grates on the sensibilities of pinch-mouthed Miss Kerr. There is something about that Look; it un-nerves her. Mr Park understands what he has taken on – his teaching career has been long and he is imbued with the spirit of advancement – and he urges the Infant Mistress to keep watch on this fey pupil with kindness.

Miss Kerr, who bears the seldom-used name of Adele, does not identify with kindness. She knows only that she is a miserable failure in the eyes of her mother, and fortunate to receive a teaching position to sustain her sorry existence. She sends most of her wages back Home to the widowed one, who had been so sure that the torturous voyage to New Zealand would procure her graceless daughter some sort of marriage. Despite the notion that any single woman would quickly be swept up and away to the marriage bed – so desperate are menfolk for a female mate – Miss Kerr's rotten teeth and associated halitosis is so bad, so violent, that any potential union is swiftly thwarted and she remains a spinster.

Oh yes, she had disgusting propositions on board the ship and a filthy encounter once she arrived, but she has no need of chastity precautions. Bitterness sees to that. Bitterness about all the forward tarts who arrive in the country with nary a brain between them but a willingness to grin and flash their bosoms and who are quickly spoken for and married. And above all, bitterness about her lot – and what better way to deploy those emotions than to berate the pupils. Make them cry, make them suffer, and if they wet their drawers or hang their head, thrash them with a cane.

Billie is always smartly dressed, thanks to Evie's innovative way with cloth and needle, and even the deep hems that may be let out in a year or two appear stylish. This affronts Miss Kerr, whose garments are exceptionally plain. Her comments are pointed: 'Well, Billie Frost, I see you think you are above us with your smart clothes'; or 'Miss Frost will show you how to calculate, since she knows it all.'

Billie does not know it all, but concentrates on her tasks while listening to older students with one ear, absorbing so much more than is allocated to the Infants. She is not overt; she knows there are always spies in the camp and does not wish to raise the teacher's umbrage more than usual. She develops a special friendship with a pupil older but smaller than herself, Temperance Ivimey. Tempe has recently arrived from the Home Counties and her voice is refined, her disposition gentle. She is not advanced, but has a way about her that transcends book learning. With some of the girls being wary of Billie's unusual stance, and a few making snide comments about Maclaggan Street, Tempe's kindness is of great comfort.

Mungo oversees Billie's journey to and from the institution. On the outward journey he trots along as she skips around the mucky ruts of upper Maclaggan Street, turns left into Clark Street and right at the High Street corner. There he stops and cocks his ragged head upward with a tender yelp and watches unwaveringly until she disappears over the hill, then turns and goes about his business. The routine is reversed during the afternoon, at a time that only he can intuit; Mungo knows his place in life is to protect his mistress.

CHAPTER
FOURTEEN

September 1864

Evie drops into the bed, exhausted from the long day's work. The last of the guests had gone upstairs by ten o'clock, but she had continued on stitching in the gentle candle-light.

She knows it is slovenly, but she is too weary to change into her nightgown, only shedding her shawl and skirt on the bedpost before crawling into bed beside her sleeping child. The bed feels like a feather cloud, even though its stuffing is only kapok. Billie murmurs in her slumbers, Evie encircles her, and knows nothing more as she falls into a long, ocean-deep sleep.

Today had started out as any other. That is, with the exception of Billie's breakfast egg sporting a pink face thanks to the cochineal water, and waxy crayoned purple eyes, mouth and hair. A chorus of happy birthday broke out. Then Mungo trotted in on cue with a small packet in his jaw and stood on his back legs in offering. 'For me, Mungo? Why, thank you, my best little friend,' and Billie tore off string and newspaper wrapping to reveal a new slate and three sticks of chalk. 'Oh, my own slate! And now I shan't have to share in school!'

'Billie, what a thought indeed! Of course you do not need to share with your classmates – ' Meg consulted Evie with a quick glance '– but surely you shall wish to share if another pupil does not have your advantage?'

Billie had looked ashamed at her outburst, saying contritely, 'Yes, Mother Meg and Alf, yes Mama. My mouth went quicker than my brain, and of course I shall share my slate.'

Then it was off up the rutted road, past the proliferation of public houses and horse yards, accompanied by Mungo to the usual spot.

The afternoon had been also like any other. Mungo had waited at his corner in a quiver of anticipation and catapulted himself forward in the usual rapturous reunion and frenzy of adoration. Then home and through the side door into the scullery for thick bread and milk before Billie's routine afternoon chores.

And the evening had continued in the normal fashion, commencing with a nutritious meal and suiting most to dine at this end of the day. Today's juicy lamb shanks, mashed potatoes and spinach from the garden was followed by jam roll with a sweet, sticky sauce and custard.

This evening's songs were, as usual, balm to the souls of their weary guests. A family of eight had begged an extra night's lodging before moving off over the treacherous hills to Mosgiel, two infants sleeping with their parents in one room and four others top'n'tailing in another. A family of five occupy the largest guest room, and two men crowd into in the boxroom barely made for one. Meg will share with nobody but her Alf, and that's that. Maguires is full and quiet except for the sounds of sleep.

Evie usually dreams of fine clothes and rich circumstances. Her recurring dream is of singing around a piano at a grand homestead before it gently transforms into a garden party where azalea petals fall all around during a wonderful sensation of floating. There are silken clouds drifting, velvet trees gently waving, and taffeta leaves fluttering.

But this time a cloud overtakes the sun and the day is becoming ruined. It is raining, sleeting and the wind is howling. Mother pulls her inside, inside to the warm of the house where the piano is playing. But the house is different, like a cave, and everyone is screaming with no sound but with ugly mouths that gush forth rivers of virulent red. Then she is being pulled from the warmth of her mother's arms and she is crying out. And this is when she awakes, gasping.

It must be a bad dream. Yes, that is it. All is well and she must sleep more to be fresh for the morning.

But the bad dream will not cease and now she is being pulled under a bridge, into a grotto, into the deepest cave. Cough, cough, she cannot breathe. Gasp, wheeze, pant. Almost choking with the lack of air. The cave's depths are pulling her down, pulling her further under. But the more she flails in its sinister hold, the hotter she becomes – so raging hot that she is thrashing off the all the bedclothes. In the distance there is barking and shouting. The smell is getting more putrid. And she really is choking.

Evie is wrenched from the sleep cave into her own dark room – but now with a sinister glow outlining the sparse features, making them look like devils and pikes. She is terrified. And she is coughing again. There is smoke billowing under the frail wooden door. Smoke and fire. Fire! FIRE! FIRE!

There is now thumping and cracking and crashing. Banging, shouting and pandemonium. Evie grabs her shawl and cries, 'Billie, Billie, wake up, wake up! We're on fire! We're on fire!' She drags the sleeping form from the mattress and across the floor. 'Quick, quick, the window!'

The sleep-drugged child clings to her mother with such ferocity that Evie can hardly stagger. She shoves Billie towards the window. She raises her arm to smash the panes, but they explode from the searing heat. Yet it is no use, the mullions are far too small to push through, and far too strong to break. Struggling and gasping, Evie tries to wrench the sash upwards – but it has been closed all winter and will not budge.

Loud screams and shouts bounce through the bedroom walls. The thin timber is ablaze and the smoke is thickening.

'Let go, Billie! Let me be so I can open the window – let go of my arm!' Evie shrieks as, struggling and panting and retching, she pummels and struggles at the heavy timber sash. It grinds apart and with a jerk is thrust upwards. More shards of glass fling down like daggers, and one plunges into her tilted neck. Panting, she pushes her head and shoulders through the opening, gasping in a lungful of night air. She hauls the clutching child upward and with a supreme effort, heaves her through the space. 'Jump! Jump!' Her voice is a croak. 'Jump, Billie!'

Slumped over the sill now, Evie glides in and out of her mind. Billie is out; she knows she must jump too. Over what she perceives to be a long, slow time, but is only a minute or two, she rouses her body enough to drag it over the ridge. Safety is coming soon. But it is so very hot, and she is so very tired, and why is it such a long way to tumble down and down and over and over to reach her precious child?

Someone is pulling her back, pulling and pulling, and will not let go. Oh, but there is Mother calling her. And there is Father, and there is little William laughing. But best of all, whispering sweet things, is her beloved sister Florence with her bonnet, bidding her to follow. Now the pulling back is being released, and the drawing forward is getting stronger.

'Come home, Eveline, come home to us all,' Florence is

calling, although there is no voice now, only a sweet hum. Or is it song? Is the bonnie boat coming over the waves?

And on a chariot of gentle memories, she floats and soars. Away, and away.

CHAPTER FIFTEEN

---~~~---

Billie's eyes slowly open. Everything is dark. Darker than when she buries her face into Mungo's soft black patches. She reaches up. Nothing is there. She rolls her body over on the hard ground and begins to crawl. One knee forward, another knee forward – but it hurts, oh, it hurts.

Mama will be cross if I get my drawers dirty. The thought hovers over her.

The dark is a little scary, but not as much as the hole under Mother Maguire's dunny seat. And then she remembers she must call it a privy. Oh, how cold it is in the privy. How cold it is, how shivery.

Her knee meets something firm. She touches, feels, and inhales the scent. And even with the reek of acrid smoke and charred wood, she knows it is her mother.

'Mama, Mama,' she whimpers. She lays her head on Eveline's lifeless form. 'Mama, don't be sad now. Courage shall not forsake us. Let us have fortitude.'

She awakens to the wan glow of dawn. She can see jagged black shapes, criss-crossed like a game of pick-up-sticks. She can see faint twirls of smoke, rising to become gathered up into the greyness that hangs over Maclaggan Street. The stench of a burnt world jags at her throat. She coughs and it feels like a wad of cotton is stuck inside her chest.

In the distance a dog barks and a few feeble responses echo back. A little later the barks come again. Then a little closer. Mungo!

'Mungo, Mungo! Here, boy – here I am!'

The hoarse yelps get more intense and joyous, and out of the vapour looms a small, singed object. Mungo, with his gammy eye and mangled ear, was never a beauty. But beauty is all Billie sees as she buries her head into him, then wraps her scorched, bruised body around his sturdy little frame; one that is waggling with such intensity that they are soon a tumble of licks and sharp cries.

Until Billie starts to choke and breaks into tight sobs. Mungo's own ecstasy reduces to a low, slow moan and they rock together until quiet comes upon them.

He stretches out and his nose touches Evie's cold form beside them. He licks and whimpers, and gives a brief shudder. Mungo has seen cold forms before and knows. He keeps vigil with Billie and her Mama as weak light filters through the haze.

Four years ago, before 'Gold!' was on everyone's lips, there were five hotels in Dunedin and now there are eighty-one, each prey to destruction from a rogue candle. This latest heap of rubble is the fifth such disaster in Maclaggan Street since the beginning of the year.

A group of grimy men poke at the charcoal and ash, occasionally stooping to retrieve an item that hasn't been roasted beyond recognition. Tankards, buckets, crockery, cauldrons lie under a heap of charred timber and corrugated iron. Silence hangs heavily over the long acre, broken by a curse, a low moan, a splintered sob, as one corpse after another is retrieved from the mangled mess. Some survivors have already been taken in by friends further up the hill, away from the stink and chaos. A lone woman claws through an area of rubble, croaking her husband's name. Two small boys kick about in the debris, happy to have something new to explore, unaware of anything more than their own world.

Into the uncanny silence breaks the sweet, liquid notes of a bellbird; then the fractured warble of a tui. Fruit trees planted further up the hill have grown to handsome spec- imens over the past few years, and terrestrial birdlife has migrated from the dense native bush to this valley. One weary forager hears the uncertain notes and turns to his fel- low man with a look that says 'out of death comes life'.

The tui's rise-and-fall stanza comes intermittently: *pip- pop, portle*. A response from deeper in the bush: *wip, tek-tek- tek, teeer*. Then the notes seem to meld into a shallow cry. A cry like a newborn, yet twisting into a croak. And the croaky cry becomes a thin wavering riff:

*'Singing cockles and mussels, alive, alive-o. Alive,
alive-o, and cockles and mussels and – '*

Intermittently it is accompanied by a reedy howl.

'Ye gods, something's bloody alive!' As if in slow motion, exhausted men start clambering over reeking rubble towards a pile of charred beams. 'Lord save us,' croaks one, 'it's a bairn!'

'Sure an' dat's no bairn – 'tis Alf's child!' shouts another. 'Jasus Mary an' Joseph – both her and da mutt are alive!'

Billie raises her eyes through the dim space above her bunker to see faces, blackened and undistinguishable. But she knows the voice of Shuran O'Fee and other gruff voices seem familiar too – friends of Alf.

Shuran's voice becomes clearer, shouting, 'Miss Billie, is it you, child? Is it yourself? Are ye hurt, oh are ye –?'

'My leg hurts something fierce, but Mungo has been keeping it warm,' wheezes Billie, 'and I've been singing and singing to keep us happy. I like "Speed Bonnie Boat" best, but he likes "Cockles and Mussels". Mama is so tired, and won't wake up. She has forgotten her skirt, she just has her shawl and petticoat. Mama must be so cold and we are trying to warm her, are we not, Mungo? And I'm hungry now.'

CHAPTER SIXTEEN

The summer days are shortening, the hillsides are warm, and the valleys accept the longer shadows. Mist hovers low over the harbour in the early dawn as the air currents merge. Dogs bark, children laugh, and without fail night follows day.

It is many months since the fire that decimated Maguire's Private Hotel, and a new building is being established on the burned-out site. But the Maguires are no longer the owners. They, along with Billie, have been taken in by the kindness of neighbours further up the hill at Abbeyleix House, one of the largest public watering holes and accommodations on Maclaggan Street. They have saved nothing – even the week's takings were consumed by the eager flames – but out of devastation there is small mercy: at least there is plenty of work available for good hotel staff.

The Maguires do have a small sum of savings with the Bank of New Zealand, thanks to their hard work and thrift, but there it shall stay; it is not nearly enough to start rebuilding. At least, Meg reminds herself, they don't live rough like many settlers, in a hut made of sticks with naught but a pan over a miserable outside fire for cooking.

Meg now works in the Abbeyleix kitchen – scrubbing, scouring, chopping, beating – and they are given lodging in return, plus a small wage. She feels comforted that they have a roof over their head, and a little extra to get by on, and she keeps her mind clear of most other concerns by being constantly busy. She feels blessed to be alive each day, and not be taken away like their dear, sweet Evie.

Not so Alf. His mind has been forever damaged by the outcome of the blaze that claimed their proud little business, but mostly by the loss of his Evie, and he cries like a baby at times. He has lost his ability to speak, and will focus on a speck of dust or a hair off Mungo, or into the distance as he sits on the hotel veranda. Shuran O'Fee comes of an evening to share a jar, and friends often drop in to play cards. While Alf doesn't partake yet, he watches and it is good therapy.

Alf will smile quietly at Meg as she strokes his hand, or prepares him for his bed. There are still some functions that he is able to reserve the right to accomplish, but on the whole Alf is cocooned in his own world. That is, until he sees his Billie, when he becomes a little more animated.

Mungo forbears her tuneless renditions, and rarely lets her out of his sight while she is in and around Maclaggan Street. She is permitted to join the establishment's guests on Friday and Saturday evenings, but never is she allowed to venture into the public bar with its rough clientele.

Billie desperately misses her mother and still weeps after her prayers at bedtime, but seldom does she succumb to excessive sadness – and indeed it is she who keeps her weather eye on Meg and Alf. Meg is busy all day in the kitchen, and Alf is hardly any trouble unless he gets agitated. His friends still bring him the *Times* and the *Witness* and read the editorial comments and snippets of what they hope will perk him up. But it is Billie who is now reading to him the most and after school, once she's completed her daily tasks, she comes to sit beside Alf and reads until he is weary. In the main he is stimulated by this activity, and from time to time he reacts with a clap or a nod or a smile that indicates the man within.

Billie learns to avoid articles that provoke too much emotion, after one such reading sent him to a lather, crying 'Fire! FIRE!' and it took her some time to calm his distress.

Her schoolwork is impeccable; she has a photographic memory, her mind is deep, and her intelligence sharp. But the infant mistress continues to resent the fact that she has a child who, at not even seven years of age, is ahead of the ten-year-olds and not far behind most of the twelves who will be leaving at the end of the year. Miss Kerr does not like children who don't conform to her standards – they confuse and frighten her. In fact, she does not like children at all, but teach is what she must do.

She refuses to acknowledge Billie other than to taunt her, sometimes with thinly concealed fury, other times with sarcasm. Whether Billie smiles, or frowns, or lowers her eyes, Miss Kerr cannot be pleased.

A few of her classmates also sneer, mainly to curry favour with their teacher, but Billie is neither brash nor falsely modest and would-be bullies don't find satisfaction. She remembers Mother's words when things get difficult: 'Be strong and of good courage: fear not nor be dismayed' and endeavours to be these things.

But she is not any keener on school, and finds comfort only when she walks with her friends or arrives home to the Abbeyleix and curls up with Alf. She is, however, keen to better herself with income, to earn extra money to help her guardians.

'God bless you, child, I would never take your money!' says Meg when the subject is broached, which it is with increasing regularity.

'Then I shall put it in the bank for later,' says Billie. 'I know where it is in Princes Street and I shall give it in there.'

'So you say, miss,' Meg sighs in defeat. She knows that this one should not get the upper hand, yet her tone is that of such reasonableness and persuasion that it is hard to resist this approach. 'But you should not expect to find work outside the domestic sort and there is plenty to do here, even if I cannot give you a coin as yet. Someday, though, I shall think of a way to spare you a penny or two, if you are intent on earning.'

'No, no, that is not what I mean at all! Oh, Mother Meg, I do so wish to get a great deal more, and I have seen those Rattray Street boys with many coins between them, and even playing flick with them.'

'Rattray Street boys? Flick? Whatever next, indeed!'

'Mother would not let me stop to talk – '

'And neither she should, God rest her soul.'

'But I do want to learn to play flick when I get those coins! How grand it would be to stack a pile on my elbow with my hand curled up just so – ' She raises an arm bent tight with an eager fist curled forward like a swan's head. 'And then – flick! – my hand would catch all the coins before they fall down, and if I should drop them I should snatch them up before the boys run and steal them!'

'Flick? Pennies? Steal? Gracious me, my Lord above, you shall not be part of that game, Billie Frost! The conversation is closed.'

But Billie's steam is now up, and during the next two weeks – carefully so as not to arouse suspicion – she slips into the curve of Rattray Street of an afternoon to watch these transactions with growing anticipation. Carriage boys they call themselves, not really urchins, mostly lads out for a chance – some toadying, others more deferential, all trying to outdo the other as boys do.

Strategy, cunning and ambition combine in a pantomime so quick that sometimes their customers are unsure of the transaction. In and out of alleys, shooed off by shopkeepers, frowned at or ignored by shoppers and passers-by, and tolerated by their hapless customers. The objective is to secure a buggy turning off Princes Street into the wide arc of Rattray Street, where smart buildings accommodate professionals in their chambers on the upper storey and merchants on the ground floor. The tactic is to appear after a shrill whistle from the corner boy and to monitor the buggy's progress until it stops and the boy who works his allocated square yards moves in: 'Greetings, sir, madam, allow me to assist you down ... take your valise ... open the door ... ' or similar lively words. And in reverse as the individual reappears from chambers, rooms or shops.

There is nothing wrong, nor is there anything right about the service; it is just another entrepreneurial scheme that does not request a fee but hopes for one anyway. For surely the act is more of a gentleman's manservant or a lady's maid, to ease their way? And if the act receives a gratuity, all to the good.

It is in witnessing this performance that Billie decides it certainly must be her mission.

'Mother Meg, you are working so hard and our Alf is mostly agreeable, and I know I must do more than go to school and come home again. You can set me more tasks here, I'm sure, but how I wish to earn some money. They say it is to be had like gold in Rattray Street where the people coming by carriage or walking to their work are helped by the boys, opening doors and such. Oh, Mother Meg, I would so love to be a door boy!'

'Hush at once, child, you shall not be a door boy. Or any boy. You are a girl, and with your lovely long hair to prove it. Be done! The subject is closed!'

The subject may be instructed by Meg to be closed, but Billie searches for an idea to convince her without incurring a ban on its development. She shall walk down to Rattray Street to consider the activities more closely. Tomorrow.

She heads up into Clarke Street the next morning as usual. But then she runs down High Street, scoots through Farley's Arcade and crosses into Rattray Street. The thoroughfare is buzzing with merchants, businessmen and ladies. She walks casually along its length and back, stops to glance into shop windows as a customer would. The boys are not overt. There are a few playing marbles which is a challenge on the sloping, rutted street, or shove-ha'penny on an improvised board, and it is not until there is a hint of business that more appear from out of nowhere and action begins.

From her casual station in a doorway further up the road Billie watches, notes and calculates. She senses herself rising above the activities, hovering and looking down upon it, the same feeling she has often experienced since the fire, and it is from this position she can analyse more easily. She finds she can keep this snapshot in her mind well after she has left the scene, which gives her the opportunity of reviewing her thoughts.

But although watching lays the foundation of how the activities take place, Billie knows it would be better to talk to a boy face-to-face. Not an easy proposition, for what rough lad would wish to talk with a girl when he has other more challenging things to do? She has assessed their personalities, at least from a surface perspective, and makes her move on a lad whose part-native face and subtle methods attract her.

She is not wrong. The boy touches his cap and answers, 'Yes, miss?' when she calls to him.

'I say, did you make some change today? I've been watching for a little while, and it looks a clever game.'

'You've been here for more than a little while, ae? Why are you hanging around?

'Hanging! No, I – yes, perhaps I have been here for a little time, haven't I? I believe the time passed quickly. But I was – I might as well say it, I was wondering how I could join you and make some coin.'

'Join us! But you are a girl and no doubt are cutting school, ae. I can see that your boots and coat aren't meant for hard graft. No girls allowed, miss,' concludes the lad and makes to move away. 'Though it is a game for most of us and better than school, ae!'

Billie has another ace up her sleeve. 'What's your name, please? And how would a boy join up anyhow? Because, you see, I know my brother wants to, and I said I'd ask about if I was passing by.'

'The name's Tama. "Passing by," you say?' and he grins with the confidence of his nine years to Billie's six. 'Well, all a boy would do is arrive on the street. Then he'd get provoked to see how he'd take it. We'd send him on errands, like to get a bucket of elbow grease or some striped paint, or josh him to see how he takes it. I'd bet your brother wouldn't be up to it, no disrespect, ae?' And the boy speeds off to assist another customer.

Billie has spent more than two hours watching and absorbing Rattray Street's busy activities. She has been here before with Mama, but even though it is very close to the Maclaggan Street gully, its fine buildings and clientele are a world away from her own. Yet there is something about this fine part of town that she is innately drawn to. She will try another day.

She skirts along into Canongate, up and up until the cottages became sparse, and cuts through into upper High Street and arrives at the schoolhouse. She pulls on her pinafore and explains to Miss Kerr that she was obliged to be of service to her guardian. In response, the bitter teacher cracks her across the shoulders with the ever-active cane, then sends her to a corner to stand for the rest of the morning. Billie hears the woman droning and chiding, and rapping at the blackboard, but no matter.

Her mind is on Rattray Street, and the way that money works.

CHAPTER
SEVENTEEN

Billie determines that her only obstacle is how to look like a boy. For two weeks she scrutinises the Abbeyleix's young guests; getting into conversation with lads is not difficult when she can offer a marble for swaps. But no lad is prepared to incur his mother's wrath by handing over his shirt and trousers. Most are new arrivals with one set on their body and the rest – if any – in trunks ready for the onward journey.

She is flummoxed for longer than she expects, though she thinks long and hard. 'Thinking it through is eighty percent of the success,' she recalls Alf saying when preparing for a session of bartering with Benjamin Solomon. Yes, Mr Solomon! She must go to Mr Solomon's shop, and see what comes of it.

Jewellery is displayed in the window case, interesting items inside the door, and towards the rear are the more unremarkable objects where she might find just the thing. But how does she pay for the transaction once she finds her goods? That, she decides, must be decided 'in due course', as Mama says – used to say. And in due course she does find worn gabardine trousers that would hold up with twine when cut off at her boots, and a flannel shirt that would tuck in well. Alf will surely have an old cap that will take her tucked-up hair and she shall weave a story for Meg so that she will cobble everything up to fit.

She weaves her tale for the pawnbroker: she is helping a poor boy who lives on her street. Ben Solomon smiles but is impervious. He only requires payment. Billie has eleven pence; the cost is three shillings.

'Three shillings? Oh, I can never get three shillings, Mr Solomon, but I can let you have –' she calculates '– let you have one half-shilling a week if you will allow me to take them now.'

'One shilling a week makes three weeks and they are yours then and not before, my dear,' replies the proprietor, used to hard-luck stories. He has a business to run, even if his friend Alf has done much trade over the years, with Billie at his side.

'One shilling a week for some poxy old clothes! No, that's far too much, but I could – maybe – pay you two shillings soon, and you will be rid of the smelly things.'

'Three shillings it is, my dear.'

'Two shillings and – and a currant loaf.'

Ben Solomon is nonplussed: the girl bargaining like an old pro, and with a look that could melt your resolve if you let it. 'A currant loaf, a currant loaf? You are a one! Well, my dear, I can't resist a currant loaf. But it will be two shillings and sixpence and a currant loaf. Do we have a deal?'

'Two shillings and a currant loaf and – ' Billie wills a solution into her mind ' – and I'll teach you how to play Old Maid.'

'Old Maid, you say? I can't resist the opportunity to learn to play Old Maid! So here is my final offer, my dear: two shillings and a currant loaf and a game of Old Maid. Are we agreed?'

'Agreed, Mr Solomon. Here is eleven pence down and I shall take the things now, wrapped up properly if you please, and it's a pleasure doing business with you.' She remembers how Alf concludes a deal.

'Ay-yay-yay!' The trader has never let an item go before it is paid up in full value. He turns and dives behind the inner door to silently release the dam of laughter that has been building up during this most peculiar transaction. He'd believed he had seen it all before, but this is one out of the box! *But*, he reflects as his convulsions subside, remembering the times Alf brought his small charge into his shop, *I suppose I could see it coming; a right little madam.* He shall say only one thing more to his customer.

'That poor boy must be very special to have such a kind bargain made on his behalf.' His dark eyes twinkle as he hands over the goods.

Billie casts hers down; she learns it is not always necessary to embroider the truth. She lifts her chin and smiles in return. 'Mr Solomon, it is you who are most kind.'

She has made thirteen pence by brushing footwear at the bottom of High Street. At one farthing for a pair, Billie has had plenty of custom and is amazed at the ease in obtaining it. She only need ask and the customers will give, but of course shoe-cleaning is a continuous requirement in this dust-or-muck town – 'Mud-Edin' as it is often known. She wonders if it would be easier than Rattray Street, but then again, sitting on an old box and buffing boots would not be nearly as much of a challenge.

It is three weeks since Billie negotiated her deal and brought the items home to be altered. She has paid Mr Solomon in full and waits with restraint for Mother Meg to finish cutting down the trousers and the shirt, and taking a tuck in one of Alf's old caps for 'a boy about my size who has none'.

Meg's weary body sleeps soundly after her long day's skivvying and she usually does not waken until 5 o'clock when it is time to get up and make her way to the kitchen. But this night something makes her wake and sit up in bed. A thief? A sleepwalker? With the ever-present memory of fire and how quickly that monster can rage through wooden dwellings consuming everything in its way, she casts her eye on the sleeping Alf and groans herself out of bed. She warily opens the bedroom door into the upper hallway. Everything appears normal; snores emanate from the bedrooms but otherwise nothing extraordinary touches her senses.

Until she sees a flicker of light under the cramped room that is Billie's, who sleeps there alone unless the establishment is packed to the rafters and another child needs a cot.

Fire! Oh, no! Please, my Lord, not again! Save us in our hour of need! Horrified, Meg hurls herself at the door and wrenches it open.

Billie is standing beside her bed with her candle flickering from its jar on the floor. *Mercy me, mercy me, all is well – only a candle flame!* But what in Heaven's name is she doing standing there with a pair of dressmaking shears up to her head and a chunk lopped off?

'What the blue blazes?! Ye gods and little fishes – what are you doing? You mad, wicked girl!' Meg lets forth a torrent of oaths and grabs the shears. She clutches Billie close and then shakes her and cries with relief and anger all at the same time.

'My hair needs to be short,' is all Billie will say, after Meg has shooed away an anxious guest and all is again calm.

'Short? Hair? In the middle of the night? I think you must be sleepwalking. There-there, oh, mercy me, you are not wicked at all, it's just a dream, there-there,' and she lays Billie down and smooths her tresses. 'Beautiful, lovely hair. To think that you were going to cut it all off! Now go to sleep, my little love and tomorrow shall be another day.' Meg returns to her bed but cannot sleep any more that night.

Billie scrunches up her mouth in review of the drama and before falling asleep herself, decides she must not distress Meg again, and shall revert to the notion of pulling her awkward mane up to fit tightly under the cap. Because tomorrow after school she shall go down to see the carriage boys.

She sets out and slips into the stables at rear of the hotel where her boy-clothes are stored; the transformation is remarkable when the roughly adjusted cap clamps up her hair. She runs down to the Rattray Street corner. From that point she walks purposefully up to a group of three boys and states, 'I would like to join you in assisting people from their carriages.'

The boys blink at her, at each other, then throw back their scrawny heads and roar with laughter. 'You do, do you? Assisting people from their carriages, ha ha. Well, sonny, you can hop it, because this here street is ours. Get away with you!'

'I should like to join,' insists Billie, 'if you show me the rules.'

'Show you the rules?' sneers one.

'I'll show you the rules!' mocks another. 'This is rule number one – ' he pokes her in the chest ' – and this is rule number two.' He pokes her again. 'Now get off our street!'

'Your street? I think not,' replies a startled Billie who, with all her bright ideas, has not thought about rejection.

'Did ya hear that? "I think not, I think not"? Oh, la-de-da I must say!' jeers a third.

'But please tell me how I may join you. I really do want to earn coin as a carriage boy and I shall only come in the afternoons to learn the trade.'

'Learn the trade? Carriage boy – what do you think of that, lads? Pipsqueak here wants to learn the trade! Ha ha ha! Now get off before I thump ya.'

In a slippery moment, more boys close in. They have all gone through their initiation and know the format.

'But I would like to join you and I shall come only in the afternoons, maybe not every afternoon.'

'Hark at it – "shall come only in the afternoons" – and what about the rest of the day, eh, eh?' Another poke confronts Billie's chest.

'Look at yer, half a jar of piss gone flat!'

'Sweetie likkle fing, betcha still suckin' on mama's titty.'

'Sooo precious! Let's see ya dance and say pretty please!'

'Go home to your stupid mama!'

Billie's senses jolt. These boys know nothing of her Mama – how dare they speak so? She will not back away now. She can hear her Mama saying, 'I daresay you shall get your way, my dear, for you don't whine and beg; you just stay fast.'

'If you will not allow me to join you and learn, then please tell me why?' she persists.

'Vis is why!' comes a roar from a larger lad who has lumbered into the fray and his hand flies at her face, intending to push but succeeding in knocking her to the ground. She lies dazed for a moment, a scarlet stream running down her pale face, while others tackle the offender and there is a buzz of dissension against him.

Slowly she stands back up, eyes clouding over like a storm coming up the bay, held-back tears producing a strange shine. Those eyes, so queerly topaz and yet so strangely flint, are on a level of the boy's chest, but they tip back fearlessly, unwavering. Tiger eyes.

'You're just a great big bully.'

'Vat's what I'm called: Bully Barnes. So if you don't 'op it – '

'A bully – with no testicular fortitude!'

'You what?! You what?! You – ah, er – '

The full impact of Billie's glare forces a disconcerted Bully Barnes to lower his own. Before his slow brain can react another boy moves to the fore. Although he is small and wiry, it is apparent by his stance and demeanour that he is not the youngest. He is clearly the leader, a posture of a young fellow.

His black hair is slicked and his eyes are like blue apothecary glass; Irish eyes. With a twisted grin he says, 'What have we here? Sure, 'tis a chancer who stands up to Bully! A turn-up for da books. What's yer name, boyo?'

'Billie.'

'Billy, you say? And how old are ye?'

'Seven. Well, seven very soon.'

'Ye've bollocks and no mistake. But come back when ye're seven and I'd say we might give ye a go. What do you say, lads? Da usual trial when he's seven?'

All boys shout the affirmative. In any case, what Tinks Toomey says is what Tinks Toomey gets.

'Actually, I'm seven – tomorrow,' Billie improvises, knowing her birthday is months away, but quickly convincing herself that this advance is only a white lie, and is for the greater good.

'Well, "ac-tu-ally" ye're a chancer, I must say, but da first t'ing you should know is, if you're after bein' seven tomorra, you orta said so! We don't want no babies around here, do we, lads?'

Tinks allows himself a haughty smile to the chorus of his minions. He then moves very close to Billie. His eyes drill down into her pale face. For the first time in her life Billie feels undone. Feels strange – not afraid – yet uneasy; daunted.

But she stands firm and her gaze doesn't waver, until he finally says, 'Bold, is it? Sure, wit' a face like yours who would argue? Let's see whacha made of, so. Report to me tomorra for me instru-chens. No, Bully – ' he extends an arm to his minder ' – I'll deal with dis recruit meself. Dis one will need partic-ilar attention.'

Billie winds her hair into the peaked cap. She wraps twine around the saggy britches and wriggles into a tight jacket over a flannel shirt then checks herself in the glass. She takes care to dress and behave like she believes a boy would do. Her role as a nabber will see her darting back and forth to the Princes Street corner, looking out for carriages turning into Rattray Street. A nabber's only job is to whistle to the so-named middlemen; they must never, ever make a show of themselves. The middlemen may shout and whistle and pander to the customers, but doormen must retain dignity; signal instructions, open doors and bow without excessive words. There is a strict chain of command and protocol amongst the carriage boys of Rattray Street.

'Sir, sir!' the middlemen call. 'Let me arrange assistance from your carriage!'

'Madam,' they implore, 'your carriage awaits. Please allow me to assist you along!'

Tama Ellison and Joe O'Malley are the current doormen, appearing instantaneously at appropriate doorways. Their middlemen and nabbers are Harold Aitken, Tommy Jory, Archie Hamilton and Tama's cousin Ariki. And now Bill Frost joins the brotherhood.

Bully Barnes glowers at the newcomer. And from the shadows, ready to initiate the recruit, slides Tinks Toomey.

CHAPTER EIGHTEEN

It is almost a year since her initial approach to the carriage boys and Billie blows on her hands in response to the autumn chill creeping up the harbour. She has endured the standard teasing and humiliation and has learned quickly. Tinks has put Bill under the guidance of Tama, whose lounging stance belies his speed when action is required. There is a slight grumbling from the ranks until the omnipresent Bully deals a punitive reward. He does not care for this departure from tradition either, but he is beholden to Tinks.

Billie is yet not permitted to open doors and bow the customers into or out of the buildings. She must only stand behind Tama – a prestigious position, although it does not pay well. After alighting from their carriage and proceeding through the door, customers who choose to tip will have already tossed a coin to the front lad and are, in the main, unlikely to present another to a small boy tucked in behind.

Most shop proprietors are not pleased to have their

frontage littered with hawkers or nuisance-makers, though some allow select carriage boys their patch. In this way there is a tacit – if grudging – agreement between merchant and boy: so long as the customers are not aggravated, the boys may continue. There are plenty of comings and goings to the shops, but the best ticket to success is ultimately the doors leading to professional chambers and offices on the upper floors. It is fortunate that there are many of these establishments in Tama's territory and in his kindness, he sometimes slips a coin to his side-kick.

She is persistent and vigilant, while some of the lads are somewhat cocky or careless and each day she tells herself she will earn more to help at home. Three times a week she hurtles down to the precinct after school, although by this time a substantial amount of custom has faded for the day. Occasionally in class she holds her breath, becomes faint and clatters to the floor and Miss Kerr says, 'Silence! I will not tolerate such disruptions, and if you are unwell go home, stupid child.' This is an ideal situation for Billie, but must not be called upon too often or run the risk of Meg learning of it. Alf has discovered her extra-curricular ruse and they have a silent agreement that he shall forget to mention it to Meg.

Mondays bring forth the professional gentlemen, and some ladies, perhaps after a weekend of debating one quest or the other; Tuesdays and Wednesdays are often slow and she does not attend; Thursdays and Fridays see the majority of shoppers. Fridays also see the solicitors and their clerks scurrying back and forth, finalising their week's instructions. Billie wishes she could work on Saturday mornings, which is also busy for merchants, but Meg definitely requires full assistance at this time. She has free rein on other days: as long as she is off to school by eight-thirty and home by six o'clock; all that she has been required to answer to Meg is that she has been helping her friends. Mother would call this a white lie, she reasons, but Meg seems pleased that Billie has made school friends. So Billie engineers her jaunts to Rattray Street on suitable days after school finishes and tallies an average of five pence for the week, mostly made up of farthings and ha'pennies.

She is promoted to share every second opportunity with Tama and starts to earn what they call a bob or two. She treasures each hard-won coin and stores it in a tobacco tin under her mattress. When it reaches the vast sum of five pounds she will present it to Mother Meg, who surely cannot then oppose such enterprise.

It all seems such a clever, well-run little earner. But Billie knows instinctively that operations which appear random seldom are.

When she has the time and inclination to do so, Billie explores the city and her guardians inherently trust her to stay safe.

She ventures far beyond Bell Hill to the north and the Exchange to the south. What a marvellous thing that the hill's bowels have undergone massive blasting and debris – tens of thousands of tonnes of it – removed pick by pick, shovel by shovel, to make an easier transition between north and south.

She would not have been so satisfied to know that the convict labourers included a group of Maori men, sent in shackles from Pakakohe after resisting confiscation of their Taranaki land by the Queen's men. And that more such slaves would be forced to follow and to live in the same abysmal, chained conditions in caves. Billie only knows that the thoroughfare is much easier than before, running north past the Octagon and the splendid George Street buildings and south along Princes Street and the many warehouses.

The Vauxhall Pleasure and Tea Gardens sound splendid and she boards the steamer *Nugget* to cross the harbour inlet. She is not out of place with couples and groups on their Sunday outings, and boards in a wave of passengers, thus saving her halfpence fare. The idea is to inspect the gardens and surprise Meg and Alf with a new attraction for them to visit on a Sunday.

Oh, what magnificence she encounters! Hot and cold salt-water baths line the jetty, one set for ladies and one for gentlemen, with elegant dressing and waiting rooms. The flower gardens and colourful borders are a sight to behold. Further ahead are strawberry gardens, and various picnic areas. An open-sided rotunda has couples dancing to an orchestra playing from the pit. The hotel has a single room: an immense chamber with a bar extending the full width, presided over by pretty ladies. Summerhouses are for hire, offering retreats for visitors seeking rest and privacy. Refreshment rooms, parlour rooms, billiard rooms, as well as archery butts and skittle alleys. And a mini zoo – cages with koala bears, kangaroos, Tasmanian devils, monkeys and a variety of birds – according to the placard, but Billie does not care for the idea of animals in cages. In wonderment she wanders until late afternoon and this time pays her halfpenny on the steamer back across the harbour. What a delightful report she shall have for her guardians!

Yet such a come-down she is in for when Meg pulls her close and says to never go there again, that the Pleasure Gardens are notorious for illicit encounters and other activities that are not nice.

Billie learns about anomalies. While clapboard flophouses and rowdy theatres, vulgar harpies and excessive behaviour are taken for granted around Maclaggan Street, the attractions of Vauxhall are a different kettle of fish.

CHAPTER NINETEEN

September 1866

Every morning except for Sundays, Edwin Northey descends to breakfast at a mahogany table laid with fine china and silverware bearing the family insignia. Breakfast is comfortably predictable with porridge oats, local eggs and bacon, toast, Scotch marmalade and good strong tea. The day that stretches forth will also be predictable with the office, the club and home again for dinner. It will the same as for many a gentleman in England – perhaps without so many amusements as English cities.

But this isn't his home in Yorkshire and the manor farm where he grew up. It isn't York with its spires and factories and new brass – with its dirt and overcrowded poverty on one hand and its inherited wealth and grandeur on the other. Nor is it Leeds with its wealthy merchants and work-house wretches. This is Dunedin, at the nether regions of

the world, full of promise but a long way from Home. It is
still difficult to call this new place home – home will always
be England, although his future will always be New Zealand.
The place is filling up with second sons, along with work-
ing-class families prepared to slog it out in a new country
and wild-eyed adventurers seeking new horizons. Plus well-
heeled, educated new-brass like himself, looking for further
opportunity. This colony is one mass of opportunity, that's
for certain and this is the sort of life Edwin enjoys. To picnic
by the ocean, to walk about in the clear air and to attend an
opera at the new Princess Theatre – all in one day – thoroughly satisfies his sensibilities.

One thing he wished to leave behind in England was
the filth of the northern textile factories and their exploita-
tion of factory workers. At first he thought of making for
India, since some of his friends seemed to have an excellent
life and income in Madras, albeit on the back of the cotton
trade – and Edwin did have qualms about the morality of
that. It was not the kind of colonialism he favoured. But
the uprisings and mutinies were of main concern and the
East India Company was looking like collapsing so he made
up his mind to head for New Zealand to join his parents
and three siblings in Dunedin. Now, after only five years,
Edwin is a junior partner in his father's law firm, where the
flood of gold and investments has produced a busy practice
and a good income. At twenty-seven he is doing very nicely
indeed and will propose to Miss Amy Barnes in due course.

Today, like any other six days of the week, Edwin leaves
home for his office. He chooses, as on most mild days, to

stroll down the Rise. As he reaches lower Rattray Street a tangle of small boys laugh and boast and toss coins from their elbows. Edwin smiles at the thought of their audacious presence amongst the more well-heeled. Indeed they do no harm, and probably some good in keeping themselves from other trouble.

His work is increasingly busy. Certainly gold is not coming in as thick and fast as it was few years ago, now that the Central Otago alluvial deposits are mostly spent. But dredging is in full force, investment in infrastructure is booming, and the stock market humming, so legal transactions always keep things busy.

Too busy actually – a gentleman who works in the city should not really work so hard, he thinks wryly. He has helped his father appoint two clerks since the beginning of the year and will have to seek another if things keep up. Clerks are not hard to come by, all educated in England or Scotland, and next year the new Otago University will be opening its doors for the first time to establish itself as New Zealand's first university.

Also, after years of non-regulation, there is a Bill before the House urging the mostly British-qualified solicitors to become certified in New Zealand's fledgling law. Edwin has urged his father to take this inevitable step and stay ahead. With Father previously of the opinion that the colonies were established by Britain and should abide by their time-honoured qualifications, he is now conceding there is a possibility for developments to be taken into consideration. He sees that Edwin is a man of the day, a man who will become more progressive over the years – as he himself had indeed done, taking opportunities as they presented themselves.

The day passes quickly and after many solid hours of work, Edwin feels the western sun slicing through his office window. He decides that he shall, for once, leave early and make the most of the late summer with his sisters and their families up the Rise. He dons his topper, buttons his coat, checks his desk once more for its immaculate state, and jauntily descends the stairs from his first-floor chambers towards the buzz of Rattray Street. Just as he is reaching for the foyer door it is pulled back by a small boy.

'Good afternoon, sir, please allow me.'

Edwin brushes past with a cursory nod and before he has time to raise his arm to signal a carriage, one of those tiresome but useful lads secures it for him. He tosses a farthing to the boy, who deftly catches the spinning coin and makes an obsequious bow. 'Insolence!' smiles Edwin to himself.

As the horse and buggy slowly moves on he glances back. The smaller door boy is now standing away from the door and is caught in full-face. And suddenly Edwin experiences the same rush of chills, the strange *je ne sais quoi* that came over him a year or so back. When was it? Yes, when he was waiting for passengers at Port Chalmers. That, too, was a child. But this is preposterous. He is seeing ghosts where there aren't any.

Over the next few days and against his better judgement,

Edwin casually looks for the lad again. Sometimes the bob of boys cannot be seen, just when one wants a carriage. Then out of nowhere, they swarm, making an intricate tableau of the process of embarking or disembarking the passengers. The game seems to start from the corner of Rattray and Princes Streets, where one urchin spies the inbound horse and buggy, and whistles to his chum on the next corner, and so on. On the outbound journey there is also honour amongst the motley gang and if that boy is still on the spot, he appears to have the right to perform again. It is a game, there must be wagers and there certainly is a farthing or more for the boy who makes the most compelling show of assisting.

Edwin smiles to himself again, thinking of his own strict but loving childhood, with little opportunity for laddish games, especially not with the village children whom he often envied for not having to be sent away to school. Although he was a good student, he hopes he will not have to inflict the inevitable harshness of public school life on his own future sons.

It is several weeks later, when the memory of the boy has faded, that Edwin suddenly sees him again, once more opening the door after he descends from his chambers to the street door. This time he stops and turns slowly and looks down at the lad. He has trouble controlling a sharp intake of breath. *What the devil – ?!*

'Sir, do you require a carriage? Here is one now, no less!'

Edwin doesn't really hear the piping voice; he just sees the face. The assured face and canted eyes. Edwin is shaken to the core. But no, he cannot – and he will not – contemplate it.

He raises his hand to his head and the boy twists away as if to avoid being struck. 'I beg your pardon,' gasps Edwin. 'I was only – '

But the child's face radiates up at him with a bright, contrite grin. 'No matter, sir. My fault!'

Edwin draws in another gasp; he again sees those amber eyes ringed with smoky grey. Like almonds toasted and salted. He sees olive skin that is at odds with the fair lashes and brows. He sees that devastating smile. 'Here, here.' He fumbles for change. 'Take this, and – and – ' He gropes for words. 'Do be careful next time.'

Great Scot! He knows now who he has seen! Alton, his younger brother. Alton, that vainglorious young swine, too charming by far and too free with his attention to the ladies. The despair of his poor parents and after too many debts and indiscretions, sent back Home out of his father's sight.

He climbs shakily into his conveyance and is driven away. Edwin doesn't see anything before him on his journey other than the ghost of Alton. He is troubled, damned troubled. Damned alarmed.

He spends many weeks contemplating the situation, knowing he must not rush at it or make a pig's ear out of what may be pure coincidence. Yet in repeatedly observing the boy, and indeed being served by him at his own door, his resolve endures. He perceives the level of command, where the young one works alongside the older in the charade: 'Sir and madam, here is your transport just arriving. Here it is, I have called it to attend. Please allow me to assist,' and so on. The passengers are deftly escorted onto the buggy then the boy confidently slaps the horse and tips a wink at the driver, who usually chooses to ignore it.

Today Edwin rejects the carriage offer and keeps walking, turning towards a shop window as if contemplating a purchase. He draws out his fob watch and checks the time but does not see it. He crosses the road and strolls back. He tries not to look at the young boy, but he must. Yet he must not – this is damned irregular. It is madness! He must do something or he shall indeed go mad.

He decides to consult his most trusted friend, James Ogilvy.

Edwin meets with James at his own rooms in Moray Place. There is no need to beat about the bush with a theoretical tale. He puts his theory and concerns direct. Then he proposes two ideas: one, that he asks the boy directly about his parentage; and two, that he follows him to his home and introduces himself.

James is astounded. He cannot understand how his usually-calm friend has put himself in such a predicament. 'These ideas are bordering on ludicrous. In any case, man, what do you hope to achieve by finding out if this is Alton's offspring?'

'Damnation, Oggers,' Edwin says sharply. He and James

have been friends since their passage to New Zealand on the same ship. 'I know one should prepare for the worst so one will never be disappointed – but this is likely to be my nephew, and on the streets begging! My brother's child! That arrogant cad, that wretched swine! And knowing his style, who knows what he's – what he's – '

'Calm yourself, Eddie, calm yourself. You are in danger of raving like a lunatic, man. At the very least you appear to be coming unhinged. I advise you strongly to treat this situation like any other: that is, with the same principles and wisdom as you would engage for a client. Detach yourself from the personal. For surely this is the best way of reaching a strategic outcome, even though we are not – at least yet – dealing with a legal situation.

'So, man to man, let us take a simple overview. Firstly, there is plenty of riffraff running around with the motive of taking one in – just look at how those boys turn a trick, if you will, for a penny. So what's to say you are not being set up nicely for a mischief? Secondly, just because you think this boy favours your brother's features, the chances of him actually being your nephew would be open to interpretation. Unless you can prove it – and if so, what then? And thirdly – hear me on this – you should not be loitering around young boys for fear of – '

'What? Good lord, Ogilvy, I cannot believe – you surely don't think –?' Edwin pales with consternation.

'My dear fellow, my fear is that you are employing emotion instead of common sense. Therefore, I urge you to consider your motives and think long and hard about them, and the potential outcomes. I beg you to not do anything for the time being. Nothing at all. Do not engage with this boy. Just think about things logically for a couple of weeks, then let us review the situation and we shall work it through clearly and without prejudice.'

James Ogilvy is sceptical: he is a lawyer. But he must do his best by his client – it is firmly established that this will be Edwin's status – and examine the full legal and moral obligations. He will not be rushed, and postpones Edwin's case for as long as he can.

The discussions are long and thorough. It is decided that Edwin will approach the lad's guardians under the guise of offering educational opportunities by way of a charity. It is not a new concept and it has a series of checks and balances. If all goes to plan he will at least be able to appease his own mind. James has advised him to tread very carefully and to accept that he is not his brother's keeper.

'Nevertheless,' Edwin has responded, 'there is something compelling about the boy – something very intelligent and far-seeing, something that should be cultured. For some reason I not only feel somewhat accountable for that rogue's doings – yes, I know, I know, it may not be so – but I feel that here is an opportunity for me to contribute to the education of this unfortunate boy. For why, if he is well cared for at home, would he be roaming the streets vying for a coin?'

'Roaming the streets – are you sure, Eddie? Perhaps the lad's just doing it for a lark. In any case, proceed with caution. Be as truthful as you can without revealing your hand. Remove your feelings from the matter, treat it with respect and with objectivity. This will give us all more time to make covert enquiries and establish a definite connection. You may gain information you wish you had never known; you may regret the whole exercise. You must proceed cautiously and I shall have your legal posterior covered at each step. One thing is clear, thank goodness – is that you will not flee to England to seek Alton out and force a duel!'

'Not at this stage,' Edwin mutters. 'No, no, don't be alarmed, my dear James, that is not what I intend. For you are quite right, quite right, the most important thing is to work quietly on the plan and its various steps of withdrawal or advancement.'

And so Edwin waits for the next time he has the opportunity to confront the boy, apparently still in partnership with an older one. And this native boy will be his initial target.

'A carriage, sir?'

'No, not this time.' He addresses the older lad. 'It's just that, er – '

'Mister?'

'What is your name, boy?'

'Tama, sir.'

'Well, Master Tama, I wish to speak with your sidekick, this young man. Good afternoon.' He directs himself to Billie. 'I think you may be someone I know. That is – ahem – I wonder if you could be the son of my friend Mr – Mr Bowles of Royal Terrace.'

Damnation! How did he ever think of such a concocted name? *Stick to the script you fool!* Edwin admonishes himself.

'Bowles? No, sir, never heard of him at all,' responds Billie with a shrug and a cocked head.

Edwin's heart thumps as he again sees the mannerisms. 'I may have been mistaken. But please, would you tell me your name?'

'Billie Frost, sir. And I'm doing nothing wrong, sir.'

'Indeed not, I was just curious. Then, may I ask, Master Frost,' Edwin rushes on to his own chagrin, 'I wonder if you know the, er, the Hepburn family who live at Heriot Row?' They are his cousins and Edwin is desperate to keep the conversation going along family lines. But he is making a complete pig's ear of it – he didn't mean to say any of this! He was going to take things very slowly, but has forgotten his lines entirely.

'I would never know anyone from the big houses up the Rise, sir.' Billie is getting annoyed, but her upbringing tells her not to be rude, especially to ladies and gentlemen.

'Where do you live, young Master Frost?'

'Maclaggan Street, sir, not far from here. But you must excuse me, I see some more chances coming my way, so ta-ta.'

Billie turns and rejoins her cohort Tama, whose only comment is, 'Be careful Bill, ae. You know what some gents are like – maybe looking for – tapu.'

Edwin stares after Billie, then collects himself. He had schooled himself on the procedure – that is, to ask more about the lad's home – but hadn't expected to be dismissed summarily. No matter, he had some information: Maclaggan Street. That hole of iniquity! That hotbed of pestilence! Always damp, like a sewer, with a stream running down it in winter; what a rotten place to bring up a child. But he shall try again at the next opportunity.

Billie is warier this time. When she opens the door to Edwin who says, 'Ah, Master Billy, just the chap,' Tama also watches carefully. At eight, Bill is still the youngest and most boys look out for each other.

Edwin proceeds. 'Now, please do not be afraid – I fear I may have startled you last time? But I only wish to ask if I might meet with your parents at some time. I do believe we might have a connection.'

'My guardians, sir, are good people and wouldn't want a fright,' says Billie firmly. 'I won't have you frightening Mother Meg or Alf. Best if you tell me directly what you want to say.'

Edwin is torn between amusement and the wish to not make more of a mess of things. 'Then, Master Billy, would you please ask your guardians, your Mother Meg and Alf, if I may call on them sometime regarding a matter – a matter that could be to their benefit. Here is my card. Please tell them that I am genuine, and do tell them there is nothing to be concerned about, nothing at all.'

CHAPTER TWENTY

Meg is uneasy. Why would a gentleman who takes a carriage from his office in Rattray Street wish to speak with the likes of them? She shall not trouble Alf at present, but she questions Billie several times to no avail, other than to be told that this Mr Northey firstly asked if she knew someone up the Rise and now wishes to visit them with regard to a matter of benefit.

Meg takes her time, but when she enlightens Alf she concludes by stating, 'I suppose it can do no harm. We have nothing to hide and we live in a public house, so if this gent wishes to sup here we cannot stop him. But I cannot meet with him until late evening, or maybe mid-morning for five minutes if I ask ahead. Let him see how he goes with that.'

And so Edwin finally arrives at the Abbeyleix and is ushered into the private parlour. He presents himself as prepared: not to seem superior, nor too servile, and ready for a raft of reactions. 'Just be yourself, Northey,' James Ogilvy had counselled. 'You are an agreeable enough chap.'

'Madam and sir, Mr and Mrs Maguire, firstly please let me thank you for allowing me to present myself in person.'

Meg and Alf exchange a silent note that although this gentleman is far from the usual patrons or individuals who visit here, his deferential introduction is not in the least patronising or awkward. Well, a little hesitant maybe. They know from experience the devious ways of most tricksters; let Mr Northey continue with his say.

'Please let me assure you that nothing is amiss, nothing at all. You have my card and can easily check on my credentials, which show me to represent Northey Solicitors. Your young lad will have told you that we have met on occasions in Rattray Street, where I have observed his intelligence.' Edwin does not want to overplay it, and his audience gives no hint of their own impressions.

'And so I am here today to introduce an organisation set up for the benefit of boys. Oh, please do not take offence.' He senses a slight jib. 'I am in no way suggesting your boy is in need of benefit in the usual sense, no indeed. But – ahem – may I continue to set out the scope of my client's organisation?'

The Maguires imperceptibly affirm, never taking their eyes off Edwin. They have assessed the introduction and are watchful of body movements and facial expressions. The words are not so important, initially.

'Thank you and – ahem – I shall begin. Firstly, I must ask of you that our discussions will remain strictly confidential, and that is on both our sides. Therefore, if you allow me to proceed, or if you do not wish me to, I must ask that for the time being, until it is agreed otherwise, this is to be discussed with no soul other than between yourselves and myself. What do you say?'

Alf and Meg look briefly at each other and give a slight nod.

'And so – ahem – to continue. My client is a charitable organisation, which is, of course, legally sound and scrupulously administered.' This is what he has instructed James to proceed with, should the initial stages prove positive. 'Its mission is, and I quote: "To educate and train boys from families in straitened circumstances, to reach and maintain their full potential and become good and useful members of society." 'Therefore,' Edwin looks up from his papers. 'this charity – '

'Charity indeed!' Meg bristles. 'We don't want charity, thank you very much! We do well enough and there're many souls that need charity more than us – isn't that right, Alf? We're not in the poorhouse yet. Charity, my foot!'

Alf nods and shakes his head and nods again and reaches over to calm Meg.

'I do beg your pardon. Let me explain that in this case the word "charity" may sound misleading. It seeks only the best – it is not a handout, not a profit-making organisation. It is run by trustees who are morally sound and whose focus is only on education. That is what I mean by "charity" in this case.' Edward draws a deep breath; he realises he has almost been holding it.

'Proceed,' says Meg coolly.

'I thank you indeed. So – ahem – to continue further.

The charity – or shall we just call it the organisation? Yes, much better. The organisation wishes to remain absolutely anonymous, just as our discussions must remain confidential. Are you agreed?'

Again a cool nod.

'So, to continue further. The organisation offers a scholarship for chosen boys, where such a boy shows above average intelligence and moreover, a character and disposition that is not so easily classified. It goes beyond intelligence. So, if you will allow me – ' Edward hears himself tending to pomposity. 'I have discovered – indeed you must know – that there is something very unusual about your boy's intelligence that speaks of the extraordinary. Extraordinary indeed. I would therefore be most grateful if you would consider my promoting your young charge for the scholarship process. Now, I am not saying at this time that anything is definite; there will some tests that need to be undertaken, tests of an academic and intelligence ratio, to assess the placement.'

Edwin feels he has stated his case well, but Meg is outraged.

'Placement? Where, indeed, would you be wanting to "place" our Billie? You can be sure we will not have the child taken from home, taken from us. Oh no, never, never!'

'Indeed no, my wording was clumsy, I do beg your pardon.' Edwin admonishes himself to slow down – to not put up details, to not speak in a way that may be misconstrued. 'No, no, please be assured, my dear Mr and Mrs Maguire, that Billy would not be taken away. Certainly not. I only mean to convey that opportunity shall be to gain placement in another school where the scholarship lies, so that Billy might study in more depth. It will be here in Dunedin; of that you can be certain.'

Meg draws in her umbrage. Alf has not made a sound. 'It is very true that sh – the child soaks up schooling like a sponge and is always reading and seeking knowledge,' states Meg. Alf nods vigorously.

'You don't say? And what does he read mostly, may I ask?' Edwin resists the temptation to lean forward. Meg is starting to thaw, although she remains upright.

'At school just her journals I expect, but here at home, sh – Billie reads the papers as much as possible to our Alf. Yes, the *Otago Daily Times* is a well-read paper here, sir. Unusual for a young'un, even at eight years old, but this began at three. Not interested in rag books like others, and what could we do to stop the child! Alfie would read a few lines, Billie would repeat them, then Alf would read them again and make an intentional mistake, then directly he would be corrected! After that it was on to reading whole paragraphs, insisting that Alf teach her new words. By six she was onto reading whole sections. Then before you could say "Jack Robinson", she was reading it alone with very few stumbles. I am sure only a portion of it was understood – not only being big words, but long-winded rubbish at times – but that child kept pressing on. Gracious, such a one!'

Meg stops herself, aware that she has rattled on, much of it the suppressed pride she feels about her ward. Previously only she and Alf acknowledge it to themselves, for who else wants to know the wearying details about others' precious darlings and how clever they are?

Edwin is rigid with interest, but endeavours to maintain a calm front. 'Reading from the *ODT* at four years old? Upon my word, extraordinary, quite extraordinary. This keen characteristic shines through, indeed, from my observations. This is the very sort of boy whom I, we – that is, my client, would wish to consider for this scholarship. But let us not race ahead! As I said, this must be taken step by step. And now, Mr and Mrs Maguire, there is another thing that must be considered. So I would like – '

But Meg intervenes. 'You will excuse me, sir, but I must take my leave – I had only ten minutes allowed for this interview and am expected back in the kitchen.' She prepares to go. 'Although you may wish to stay a while to share a porter with Alf, but you must not upset him, is that clear? His nerves are affected and you must not agitate him.' Meg would not usually talk to a gentleman in this way, let alone a legal gentleman, but where Alf is concerned she is fiercely protective.

'Indeed, madam, and I thank you very much for hearing me out thus far.' Edwin rises and assists Meg. No chance to inveigle further information on the child's background, but steady, old boy, time enough. 'Mr Maguire, sir, a whisky or a porter?'

Alf nods at the two suggestions and the proprietor pours his standard Scotch and chaser. Edwin likes this chap, solid working class, and with a way of expressing himself by facial expressions and hand movements. Alf gestures to his favourite table, north-facing to soak in all the available sun, and removes the *Times* from it.

Edwin sees an opportunity. 'I say, should you like me to read to you –?' And immediately knows he has overstepped the mark. 'Ah, I do so apologise. I wager you still read yourself very well?' He meets Alf's smiling eyes. 'And your lad reads to you and you just take it all in, so as to encourage him? I like you, sir, I like you indeed! If I had children, I would hope to be such a father.' And he fervently hopes that these comments are not taken the wrong way.

Alf is not concerned. He likes the man – genuine, although somewhat nervous. Perhaps he just has a nervous disposition; it doesn't appear to be sinister or cunning.

Three more long weeks tick over before Edwin manages to secure another such meeting. He gets straight to the point after the initial pleasantries and is less nervous.

'At our last meeting I referred to the possibility of a scholarship. What are your thoughts on the matter?' Meg indicates they are interested in more information and he proceeds. 'Forgive this intrusive line of questioning – that is, getting a little more background information – but next I must ask about your boy's background prior to your becoming guardians. It is just a formality, but one which is important,' Edwin holds his breath: *Please Lord, don't let me sound condescending.*

The Maguires are not ignorant. They know that there is such a thing as scholarships, although no person they know has received one. They have little knowledge of education here in New Zealand, other than the fact it is not compulsory. Nor is it free, except in the missionary schools for natives. But why else would they have emigrated other than to bestow on their future children – and now it is only Billie – the very best of every opportunity? They have agreed, after nights of discussion in their own way, that if this so-called scholarship that has landed out of the blue into their lap can lead their Billie into the best path, they must take advantage of it.

They know that checks will be made on their own authenticity as guardians and Meg tells the practiced story of Billie's appearance into their little world. Tells of a young lady's plight with a new baby and how she seemed loath to reconstruct her past. Tells of the furs and the fine boots. Tells of how she was Eveline Frost, so called, who named the infant Billie. And then, quietly, tells Edwin of the tragedy that claimed the mother's life and their pledge to bring the child up as their own.

'Fire, fire,' whispers Alf, but not in distress.

Edwin fixes on the name Eveline Frost and quietly records it. He at last has a clue about the mother that he may be able to pursue without distressing the Maguires. He records names, dates and milestones and systematically proceeds with his proposal regarding the future education of the remarkable child.

'He will be educated by outstanding teachers so that when he matriculates and goes on to university he is in front of the pack, so to speak, and able to get on in the world.' Meg and Alf gasp loudly at the astounding idea of university.

Edwin reacts and pauses. 'Ahem – but I am getting ahead of myself, please do excuse me. Today I only wished to talk about the concept of the scholarship and a new school, and your permission to take the matter to a legal basis and the next step. At this point are we agreed?'

Alf reaches out and shakes Edwin's hand most vigorously, but Meg is slower in rising. She takes Alf's arm and he pats her hand as she looks squarely at Edwin. 'All well and good,' she says. 'Should our Billie prove to meet your conditions we should be pleased to talk about it further.

'But there is one other thing, sir, that you must know.'

CHAPTER
TWENTY-ONE

———— ~∽~ ————

Edwin is having difficulty getting over the shock of it. His brain feels mangled. The boy – the boy who looks exactly like his own brother – is not a boy at all. He is a girl! Preposterous! Hellfire and damnation, how the Dickens didn't he pick it? And what in the blazes does one do now! He hasn't handled it at all well, stuttering – to the amusement of Meg and Alf – that, um, he shall have to, that is – a girl?! Impossible!

But not impossible, it seems. All he can do to acquit himself is to say he shall need to consult with his colleagues and shall be in touch in due course, as he endeavours to keep himself erect while bidding farewell for the present.

And now he is back with James Ogilvy, who in turn is amused at the whole charade. 'Damn it, Northey, what a superb act! What a farce! To possibly be your brother's offspring is one thing. For the lad to be from the slums is another. But for him to turn out to be a "her" takes the cake! Ha ha ha! What a wonder! But steady yourself, old man – here, have another dram to settle your nerves. That's the ticket. Oh, ha ha, I'll be damned!'

He tips back his own whisky, still chortling. Then shrugs his coat lapels to order and forces himself to continue in a serious vein. 'Now look here, I shall challenge you as you would me in a matter of consideration: What is the difference, I say? If you were prepared to take on that scoundrel Alton's bastard child – yes, I say, that bastard child – why should it matter if it's a male or a female? Think on it, man, think on it!'

And so James Ogilvy trumps his friend Eddie Northey – he who claims to be a forward thinker, a planner for success – who certainly has not taken this factor into consideration. But when he has had time to recover from his high amusement, James knows it is a proposition for much more thought. For what, indeed, has he and like-minded men come out to this far-flung colony for, but to take every opportunity that presents itself? This, clearly, is an opportunity to back a novel proposal.

Edwin stares gloomily into his whisky, now fully realising that he is hoist by his own petard. It takes him some time to wrestle with the flawed outcome of what he thought to be his progressive philosophy, and his altruistic notions for the boy. But not a boy – a girl! So be it: good may yet come of it. Let himself be advised. Let himself be a willing champion of the future.

He takes a deep breath and smiles wryly at James. He has

had one devil of a shock, but the world is galloping forward – and he shall go with it! And, by Jove, next week he shall even propose to dearest Amy! He shall regain composure, look forward and be in good heart for the future.

CHAPTER TWENTY-TWO

February 1867

With much deliberation the Thornbury Scholarship is set up, Edwin choosing the name in remembrance of his Yorkshire home. He remembers the onus as a first son to represent the family's future and how his father had set great store by land holdings, with the advantage they gave over those who did not own such.

He remembers Father's face in confidently announcing that his family would be sailing for New Zealand. Edwin did not know at the time that his father's cotton mill investment had suffered badly and that he believed the best way to recoup his losses was to lease the Thornbury estate and establish ventures where sound money was to be made – the colonies. He remembers how his mother and sisters had cried but Father had remained adamant. Tied to his law clerk job, Edwin had bid farewell to his family at the London docks, but had followed them out to Dunedin some three years later.

The Thornbury estate is still safe and sound, as far as he is aware, now that it is back under family management. Alton is overseeing it all – well, enough about him at the minute, thinks Edwin, or I shall become distracted. At least its financial reports have always been satisfactory,

The scholarship documents are settled and Alf and Meg are – after much discussion and intelligence that astounds and enlightens the higher-educated Edwin – reasonably well satisfied.

When Miss Kerr receives the news that Billie Frost has transferred to Middle School in York Place she is vastly relieved. She has had palpitations every day since this child presented at the infant department. Too clever by far. Those bold eyes looking right into her very soul. That way of letting things flow over her head. Blasted little devil. How delightful that the brat's very presence will no longer be around to irritate her.

At Middle School, Billie encounters a form of teaching she has not previously known. Miss Mary Clayton is firm but kind. She challenges her students and requires more than rote learning and yes-no answers. She demands that they be accountable. It is amazing for Billie, who has previously curtailed her mind during school hours. She moves swiftly through the curriculum, plus the extra projects set by her teacher. Mary Clayton is suggested by some to be 'too pretty to be a school ma'am' and by others to be 'tending towards sedition'.

She talks of the continuing Maori Wars now carving their way through Taranaki in the north. The skirmishes between tribes can be understood and it is a moot point that some are peacemakers and others are savage. Bloody massacres are still taking place between settlers and natives over the confiscation of Maori land. But why would settlers not be told the truth about the acquisition of their proposed packet of land before embarking on their hopeful journey to the Antipodes? Colonisation and submission, conquer and rule – this has been the way of the world since time immemorial. And yes, that is the premise of the Treaty. But it does not sit well with Mary Clayton and in a careful way she presents her opinions for her students to consider.

She is undeterred by criticism of her views and to date the Inspector has found nothing but bright children who gain high marks in the curriculum. Mary Clayton is fond of quotations, which she writes on the blackboard.

'*Shall I be wrong, or shall I tell the truth?*' Helen of Troy – how stirring.

'*The next best thing to knowing something is knowing where to find it.*' Samuel Johnson – that's great advice!

And the one that sits so well with Billie's own restless mind, from Shakespeare's *Hamlet* '*To thine own self be true.*'

Miss Clayton encourages all pupils to read the library of books she has acquired over many years, and to discuss them. How deep are the Brontë sisters' words, how grim are Thomas Hardy's settings, and how exciting are Jules Verne's speculations! Miss Clayton summarises the story first, then lists scenarios on the blackboard and students vie to guess how it comes together and what it all means – marvellous!

There are thirty-five pupils in the standards classroom, quietly drawn in by the teacher's methodology. The three boys at the front who cannot sit still are delegated tasks to keep them in hand as much as possible; contrary to normal classroom procedure, the rod is not used on these lads. Miss Clayton never raises her voice and although she moves graciously between the aisles and rows, she seems to appear at any given spot like a genie, at the precise moment of need. Here, learning is on another level and not all levels are according to age. In the morning Billie speeds through the set syllabus – the Education Board is determined to implant the best educational practices of Scotland into Otago – and absorbs higher learning during the afternoon.

She has left the group of carriage boys now – told them, 'I'm going to another school further away and classes finish too late for me to come now.' The boys were philosophical about her departure although Bully Barnes mocked, 'Too good fer us now?'

Tama gave her arm a comradely twist, 'Kia kaha, Bill – be strong.'

Tinks Toomey merely said, 'good luck, so'. Then, as she turned to leave, he swung towards her ear and whispered, 'Miss.'

It is at Middle School that Billie makes a new set of friends – friends who don't scoff at her abilities. They are sisters Sophia and Ellen Erridge, Ralph Nathan and Benny Hallenstein. The five of them are intelligent and competitive and Billie's spirits fly as high as her education. She can't wait to go to school each morning and she can't wait to arrive home and give a dissertation on her day.

Chilblains continue to claim her fingers and toes between June and September, despite strong boots and thick mittens. When Miss Clayton suggests Billie should board with her family during the worst winter snaps Meg is up in arms at the suggestion. How can she sleep without her beloved child safe in the adjacent room?

Alf strokes his whiskers and ponders and pats Meg's worries into logical shape. Hasn't their darling child been seen crawling of an icy morning up the steep and slippery Stuart Street, scraping along, two steps up and one skid back? Don't her chronic chilblains send her nearly demented with itching and scratching? Isn't the light snow treacherous when it thaws, then freezes over, creating the potential for a nasty fall?

Meg reluctantly agrees that Billie may accept the invitation for the most gruelling days of the winter freeze. Billie is overjoyed at the prospect of boarding with Miss Clayton – there are surely so many more books to read after her homework is completed. Books that Mary Clayton will not bring to the classroom.

Billie is nearly ten years old when the prospect of 'extended education' is raised. Edwin Northey has discussed it with James Ogilvy, who must in turn discuss it with his senior partner, his father. Joseph John Ogilvy takes considerable convincing that a female should enter his chambers. A boy clerk perhaps, but never has he heard of such an arrangement for a girl.

'Look here, Father, this girl is every bit as good as a boy, if not better, and she has meticulous arithmetic and spelling. Not that – ' he sees horror pass over his father's heavily whiskered face '– we would consider employing a young one in such an activity. I merely thought that we could employ a cadet and lead the way for cadetships.'

'Cadetships? My dear boy, as you know New Zealand law is still based on the laws of England. J. J. Ogilvy reaches for a leather-bound tome. 'The English Laws Act stipulates, and I quote: "The laws of England as existing on the 14th day of January 1840, shall, so far as applicable to the said Colony of New Zealand" – etcetera, etcetera – "shall continue to therein be applied – "

'Therefore, I do not see how a "cadetship", as you call it, relates to the law and therefore to our business.'

'Pardon me Father, I take your point, but my thinking is that law does not enter into it at all. My thinking is about a new idea – '

'Not enter into it? New idea? My dear boy, all we do is carry out the practice of law to the best of our sworn abilities, not follow the vagaries of new ideas! And the proposition of a female – that is quite out of order.'

'I take the opportunity to challenge you on that, Father. What I see is an administrative situation, not a legal one. I find it damned difficult to carry all my papers to and from the court. I find it damned difficult to stack and store all our papers tidily. And I must say, Father, I find it rather – er, dusty in here and would welcome a cadet to – to tidy and so forth.'

James Ogilvy is at once ashamed of himself – this is not at all what he was going to suggest. He has warmed so much to Edwin's outrageous idea of introducing Billie Frost to the peripheries of commerce and law, that he is now as keen as if it had been his own. There was no suggestion she should be a skivvy, collecting dust balls off the stairs.

'Dust? Just dust and tidy?'

'Perhaps initially, Father. It would be a good way of your assessing whether the idea would work.'

'An idea has no place in a law practice, James. No place at all. But let me think on it. Now: I presume you have plenty of proper work to attend to?'

It takes some time before Mr Ogilvy Senior responds further. James endeavours to bring up the issue, but is not to be satisfied. It is only after several weeks have lapsed that his father calls him in, directs him to sit, and begins in his usual laborious way.

'Insomuch as I have given a great deal of thought to

the situation; and whereas I have considerable difficulty in allowing it; and ... '

Etcetera-etcetera, breathes James as he maintains his usual agreeable countenance.

'... most irregular ... therefore ... in this instance ... we shall give it one week's trial.'

James gives a start. He has not expected this response. 'Oh, yes, Father, that is splendid, splendid!' But he is stymied by his father's upturned hand.

'This – ' Ogilvy Senior signals to a document ' – is the list of conditions to which you will agree. Or not, as the case may be. Since you are a partner you are entitled to your view, and for that view to be considered seriously. You have not undergone your studies to be engaged in 'new ideas', but I trust your judgement – on most issues. However, this is not a legal matter, it is a personal proposal, as I am entitled to give.

'You will see, as you read in eagerness of such "new ideas", that it contains restrictions including: one week's trial for your purpose only; dismissible immediately at any time thereunto for whatsoever breach I consider to be relevant; no babbling or extraneous noise; no clattering on the stairs; never, ever to enter my office; never to hear any client business or to witness same; to receive no recompense; thereafter to be considered for a further trial of two weeks under the same conditions. Thereafter that we shall have a further discussion.'

James is slightly deflated but hardly surprised. His father is a hard man, and to concede to this point shows James there is ground to be made. 'Thank you sir, and I shall do my best to ensure you are not disappointed.' He wonders if he is, by nature, likely to be as innovative as Edwin. He shall inform him immediately!

Billie is confirmed into her Wednesday afternoon position as cadet. It is not gruelling for her to remain quiet while tidying, listening, observing; she is quite able to be a chameleon.

After three months, J. J. Ogilvy cannot fail to recognise the bright and clean conditions – with the exception of his office. The stairs are less dirty from street dust. Documents are neatly tied and pigeonholed. Writing paraphernalia is laid out precisely on desks. Books are stacked cleanly or returned to cabinets.

'Hmmph,' is all he will say. He never needs to witness this ghostly addition to his staff – on Wednesdays J. J. plays golf on the Caversham flats. With three others, all solid Scots like himself, he is working towards select membership in order to form the first Dunedin golf club.

At midday each Wednesday Billie now speeds from school to Moray Place, where she quickly accomplishes her office tasks, then collects her satchel and accompanies Mr James Ogilvy on his walk to court.

She walks briskly beside him, listening to his mumbling preparations and his observations of the journey. She is neither a clerk nor an onlooker, neither a companion nor a servant. She is just Miss Frost, a peculiar arrangement, but one that satisfies all concerned. The arrangement is, to Billie, as exciting as her former occupation of carriage boy.

'Do you enjoy your Wednesdays, Miss Frost?' James asks one day.

'I do, sir, certainly, but not the office stuff so much.'

'Not the office? But you are so tidy and precise, at least from what I see, and when I want something I can either find it or you put your hand on it directly.'

'That is so, that is so.' Billie has picked up some ponderous expressions. 'But I much prefer the buildings. The buildings as we pass to Court. And its handsome scrolls carved on the walls, and the beautiful polish on the bannister, and the rugs – I just love to squish my fingers through them.' She chatters on until, 'Oh, and of course I am helping you, Mr Ogilvy, helping you think about those naughty people who try to diddle the system.'

'Diddle the system? Good Lord, what an extraordinary description. So be it, Miss Frost. There are many who try to diddle the system, as you say, and we are about to embark on a new case of swindle. I cannot say too much, but you will no doubt watch with interest.'

James is as intrigued with this unusual, persuasive child as others have been before him. To the devil with convention. As long as she keeps up her tasks, keeps out of Father's way and keeps matters to herself, she shall remain his quaint young cadet.

CHAPTER
TWENTY-THREE

September 1870

Meg, Alf and Edwin raise their mugs of ale on Abbeyleix's first-floor veranda, toasting the tepid late-winter sun and Billie's twelfth birthday. Edwin has become more than a business acquaintance and from time to time he visits for pure enjoyment. Today they look down over the stables forecourt where Billie and her four school cohorts play a loud and laughter-filled game of blind man's bluff. She is quick at identifying the player once her sensitive fingers chance on one, but quite hopeless at the game, staggering and bumping about. A sense of direction is certainly one talent Billie Frost does not have, but she will not surrender.

Luckily her other talents are many and her love of textiles has developed an appetite for fashion and design that is becoming as keen as her mama's was. She cannot sew – all the stitches are awry – but this is where her friends Temperance and Sophia are called into action. Billie spends time at the end of her day sketching daring styles. How Alf laughs when she draws men in tartan knickerbockers and knee boots. How Meg shies when she views the enormous, feathered hats: 'I'd need meat skewers to keep those contraptions on!'

Billie's figure drawings are more like a swash of movement, yet they deftly convey the human form. Tempe and Sophia are as keenly interested in style as Billie and wish to own a shop that supplies beautiful clothes. Billie does not wish to own a shop, but is interested in supplying it with her talents. 'And we might earn a hundred pounds a day!'

She completed the middle school curriculum before she was eleven, but stays on with her contemporaries under Miss Clayton. Middle School has outgrown itself, and is now newly housed in Arthur Street.

Billie is not considered different by her fellow pupils, other than the strange fact that she enjoys extra tuition, and she engages with them in her usual outgoing way. They will all progress from Arthur Street School at the end of the year. Some boys will go on to work and some to Otago Boys' High. Some girls will stay home with their mamas and the fortunate few will continue with private education, or even go on to secondary school.

The new Provincial High School for Girls is to be estab-

lished next year after six years of petitioning by Miss Lear-
month Dalrymple and her associates, including Mary Clayton and Amy Barnes. Encouraged by Provincial Treasurer
Julius Vogel, the dauntless band of women advocated the
view that girls deserve more than embroidery lessons and
singing tuition designed to help them attract suitors. 'Intel-
lect is of no sex', claim the petitioners, to the horror of those
who believe the very word exemplifies debauchery. But at
last girls will be able to achieve more than learning how to
balance a book on their head and make calming conversation, through the opportunity of a more rigorous academic
education.

Edwin's plan is for Billie to have this opportunity, but
not immediately. After conversations and general opinion
at dinners, he feels it will take a while for protocols and
directions to settle down. For one thing there is not yet a
building fund and the girls will initially be taught in one
of Boys' High classrooms. For another thing, for all his forward thinking Edwin is not convinced that girls will do
well in a mixed, higher-educational environment like their
American counterparts. Not that the sexes will be taught
together, but their physical proximity in the initial buildings may take the focus off learning. He feels that Billie's
education should not be subjected to the trials and tribula-
tions of a new school, despite his admiration for Miss Dalrymple. Instead she should be engaged productively for a
while yet.

After that perhaps she may be ready – and may be permitted, at not yet thirteen years old, to enter straight into

the fourth form, where she will no doubt mix with a wide range of academically-inclined girls and go as far as she can.

Meanwhile, he proposes that Billie does not go on to high school at its outset and her guardians deliver this news.

'But I want to, I want to go!' she cries with a flash of fury. 'I want to go and be able to kick about!'

'Kick about indeed, miss. There will surely be no kicking about at all. We are talking about a high school and you will remember that you are privileged to be able to apply,' Meg states sternly.

'Oh, how I wish I were a boy – and I have never done so before. But I shall, I shall go on to learn more and more!'

'A fine passion you show, but Mr Northey thinks otherwise at this time and you have been very pleased with his suggestions to date.' Meg struggles to be firm. 'Yes, he does hope you will go, only not at this time. So for next year you shall probably go on with Miss Clayton.'

'I do love Miss Clayton, certainly. Only, I think it would be marvellous to kick about with high school girls.'

'Kick about, indeed!' says Meg once more.

And I shall, thinks Billie. Alf glimpses the Look, smiles and gently pats his wife's arm in the long-familiar way.

Now the young ones are exhausted and dusty. With flushed faces and eager bellies, they are agitating to come inside for their afternoon tea of bread and jam, cake and ginger beer. Edwin has acknowledged Billie's opinions on high school. He has watched, thought and reflected on where to from now. As he descends the main stairwell and joins the flurry of youngsters in the private parlour Edwin decides it is time to consider a new direction.

Billie could be a real leader; a leader of her time. Not only shall she have a secondary education, she may even be able to go on to university one day. Although the prospect is well into her future and tertiary education for girls is not yet on the statutes in New Zealand, Edwin believes she would enjoy the challenge. The notion is not outrageous; Sweden and America have been producing college-educated women for years and now England has joined the ranks. Thinking far ahead, of course, but perhaps he can find a way for her to sit the first scholarship examination to be introduced by the University of New Zealand next year. He will think on it further. He will make investigations. Yes, yes, he must scope Billie's future carefully.

As Edwin strolls along Princes Street early that evening with Miss Amy Barnes on his arm – they are bound for the Theatre Royal and have alighted the carriage some way before so as to take exercise – he is alerted to a din outside Wain's Hotel. The stagecoach from Central Otago has just arrived in a flourish of whinnying and clatter.

'Make way for Ned Devine!' smiles Edwin and proprietorially soothes the slim hand of his companion who is not in the least startled by the commotion. 'Such a showman, but a capital chap indeed. We've done business many times. I'd trust Ned with my life – even if he is an Australian!'

CHAPTER
TWENTY-FOUR

When Edwin proposes that Billie should have the opportunity to travel around Central Otago by stagecoach from mid-January next year, Meg is horrified. Why in heaven's name would anyone go on such a dangerous journey if they didn't need to get to that part of the world for any good reason? The tracks are fraught with hazardous slips, the rivers flood in a moment and drownings are rife. They believe the drivers are extremely uncouth and the carriages vastly overcrowded. Murders are said to be commonplace. And just last week they heard that a posse of gunslingers – mad, pistol-packing bushrangers – shot a driver who refused to disembark, leaving him and his escorts to freeze to death overnight in the gully.

'Dangerous and unnecessary – I doubt it very much, Mr Northey, sir!'

But Edwin presses on. He explains his plan, that Billie

would be strictly chaperoned by his good friend Angus Macandrew, Esquire, who makes the journey regularly to inspect the Bank of New Zealand branch offices. His business is not connected with the gold escorts, who travel separately and do face the possibility of stickups. Also, he and Macandrew know some of the Cobb & Co coachmen. One Mr Devine is the best in the business with an excellent record and arguably the finest skills: indeed, he recently turned his carriage's rear wheel on a half crown for a wager outside Wain's Hotel! The gold rush is dwindling, most prospectors having moved on to Nelson and the West Coast and the threat of outlaws and stickups is much lower these days. In any case, robbers target the gold escorts, not passenger coaches. Yes, the Yankee and Aussie whips are the best, superbly skilled and experienced and Macandrew chooses his ride accordingly. And as for that story about the gold escort being left to perish – well, it was surely put about by one of the other coach competitors.

'Outlaws! Stickups! Yankees! My dear Lord, I thought I'd never see the day when any travel was worse than our journey across the seas all those years ago!'

Meg is faint at the thought of the entire prospect. It is surely improper for a young girl to be traipsing off on a six weeks' tour of the goldfields, or indeed to be travelling alone with a man.

Edwin knows he has glossed over the potential dangers, but he has made the journey each year without incident and Angus Macandrew does his circuit every six months. The likes of One-eyed Jimmy, Captain Moonlight and Bully

Hayes need not be drawn attention to. He must gently press the point about how clear and clean the air is, how Billie will be closely chaperoned, and how much she will learn.

It takes Meg several weeks to come around to the notion of Billie coaching around the gold trails. Edwin assures them the journey will not only be safe, but Macandrew is a very respected gentleman, whom they shall of course meet – together with his wife who will assure them of her husband's honour and attention to his duties. He is also likely to bring his son as he does from time to time. This venture will be a great educational opportunity for Miss Billie.

'Educational? How is she to be educated if she is kept away from her schooling?' frets Meg, but Alf makes a wide smile now and nods.

'Indeed, Mr and Mrs Maguire, Billie's education is very much in my mind. She will see and absorb an astonishing amount of education by watching the process of commerce in this manner and I am sure she will be delighted to have the chance to do so in another geographical environment. She will stay only in good quality accommodation where the proprietors are of excellent character.'

Meg acquiesces; what good would it do to forbid and deny? No doubt there is nothing new under the sun and females of ancient times may well have done similar things! She tries to convince herself not to worry and says, 'Alfie, why am I taking on like this? We know our Billie will do what she will – although she is a sweet pigeon, she will get her way in the end. I daresay I am like any mother who frets on their children. So Meg Maguire,' she commands herself, 'you shall now stop mithering and let Providence protect our beloved daughter.'

'Fire,' agrees Alf calmly.

Billie is ecstatic at the prospect of the next few months' adventures and hopes she might have a Yankee driver, one who has fearsome tales to tell of the Wild West. She hopes she might encounter a gunslinger, a daring and masked highwayman who shouts, 'Stand and deliver!' He will have flaming blue eyes and only rob those who deserve it, and no doubt give it to the needy.

Stand and deliver – how marvellous!

PART TWO

CHAPTER
TWENTY-FIVE

Monday 23rd January 1871

Meg is unable to farewell the coach at daybreak – her kitchen duties will not allow it, or more truthfully, she cannot bear the thought of it. She clutches her child tightly and Alf gently disengages her after a time, before shouldering Billie's trunk and with Mungo as a natural choice, accompanies her to the Wain's Hotel dispatch. Alf strokes each of the six matched greys and admires the gleaming red coach with its scrollwork and distinctive yellow wheels, all strong and light, with leather through-bracing and powerful brake. Billie clambers up the footstep after hugging Mungo and her guardian. 'Hurrah, hurrah and ta-ta for now, Dunedin!'

Women squeal as 'Cabbage Tree Ned' flashes a wide smile and cracks his whip over the leading pair who whinny and perform a mock shy. He may be an expert on the reins, but Ned Devine is also a dandy with his well-oiled hair, tight Bedford cord trousers and heavily braided velveteen coat.

Billie waves excitedly but is cramped between two men and two elderly ladies so is unable to secure much movement on the plush seats. She faces Mr Macandrew, his wordless son and three others, cramped in like sardines and some of them nearly as odorous. 'There are ten of us inside this coach, never mind those on top, so we shall need to take small breaths,' she instructs them all, 'by crikey!' She heard that expression from Cabbage Tree Ned earlier, and it zings in her mouth like sherbet powder.

Passengers exchange glances as if to say, 'Let's hope this prattle doesn't continue.' Some smile benignly, others feign deafness. Public transport is an event to be endured.

The laden coach pulls away from the departure point with a surplus of shouting and whip-cracking, and the six-in-hand advance at a steady trot through the northern streets. They pick up speed, not slowing as they ford the shallow waters of the Leith. Now into a gallop and on to Blueskin without a minute to spare, given the manner in which the whip encourages the horses.

Two of the passengers are sisters, dressed identically and so alike that they could be twins. The Misses MacGregor smile continuously and nod and finish each other's sentences without pause. They look at each other for approval and never does the other fail to give it. They look dotingly upon Billie and undertake to watch out for her.

Refreshments are taken at Carey's Hotel while the team

is changed, then they are off on another two hours of rolling and pitching before skidding to a halt at Waikouaiti. Three travellers change to a coach-and-four bound for Oamaru and the remainder stop only for five minutes.

It is time enough for Billie to make the acquaintance of a girl her own age who is to travel with her parents and small dog Kip. 'By crikey Susannah,' she says, 'I daresay it shall be refreshing not to hear again that the fare to Waiko'ite is only twenty-five shillings, whereas it's sixty shillings to Oamaru. Or to have to endure that frightful pong!'

With an addition of the new passengers, including an Oriental gentleman in a top hat, the rollicking pace progresses them onwards once more.

By the time they are well into the hills, the horses are panting heavily. Before they start on the next sharp ascent the passengers are requested to disembark and walk a while. The male members walk ahead with Ned and one brake man. The second brake plods some yards behind the carriage, on the lookout for back-slips. The women and young ones bring up the rear. Every now and then Ned calls a halt so the horses can take a breather and the laggers can catch up and rest.

It is on one of these breathers halfway along the Pigroot, that Kip starts to bark hysterically. The terrier yelps and tugs and breaks free of its berth behind the box seat then leaps off the coach. It scrabbles in the dusty shale then speeds off towards the west, and the travellers see that it is chasing a black object running for its life through the yellow tussock landscape.

The object is agreed to be a cat, some having gone feral over the years after escaping from domesticity and becoming lost in the hills. The feline's speed is remarkable as it arrows straight ahead without a tree in sight to clamber up. Then it suddenly dummies wide, bounds in a glorious pattern over straggly clumps of purple thyme that cling to the dry earth and doubles back to head for the coach, apparently perceiving that its only chance of safety lies in mounting one of the front horses. The maddened cat leaps onto the tail of one of the leaders and fastens its claws deep within its hindquarters. The horse and its leading mate tug and thrash within the shafts, trying to break free.

Ned Devine lashes and lashes at the cat from his position of control. 'Hell's bells and buckets of blood! Get off, you bloody bugger, get off, I say! Whoa, whoa, whoa Beauty, whoa Lucy!' but this exertion does not calm the horses who are tugging and wrenching. The cat, its bulging eyes full of fear and fury, squalls louder and digs further into its hold, before it finally disengages itself and sprints for the hills.

But the damage is done and Ned Devine is furious. 'Hell's fire! You crazy bloody mutt!' The latter oath is directed at Kip, who has given up chase and is limping and whining around his owners. 'Strewth! The shaft's cracked through and the through-brace has fair ripped into Beauty's rump with her tormented jumping – what a stupid bloody dog!'

Its owner steps forward to protest. Ned raises his whip and the man cowers and the women gasp, but Ned only lashes the ground several times and stamps and paws like the horses.

Then he draws in a deep breath, slaps his corded thigh, throws back his great head and laughs loud and long. 'Bugger me days, folks! Wouldn't that rip ya nightie? That cat gave us what for, hey what? Gave us what-for! It's enough to make a stuffed bird laugh. Okay, okay, show's over – let's get to work now, men!'

Ned Devine releases the horses to graze as he sets about treating the gallant lead pair's wounds and lashing up the cracked shaft.

Billie jumps up and down clapping, but the two Misses MacGregor clutch their breasts and each other in rapid succession. 'My dears,' cries one sister to Billie and Susannah, 'that you should hear such words!'

'Such words!' agrees the sister and totters backwards inhaling deeply. Whether the deep breath causes her to take in too much oxygen or whether the thought of such words penetrates her modesty, she slumps to the ground in a faint.

At the same moment the carriage, now free of the horses and much lighter, starts to drift backwards. Before anyone can gather their senses it gains momentum and the inner wheel catches one leg of the prostrate lady before it comes to halt against a rock. Then, slowly as if caught in time, the whole thing topples sideways. The whip and his men lurch forward and grasp at the rear wheels and just manage to halt its downward trajectory.

'Fuckin' bloody son of a bastard!' roars Ned Devine at his brake, who has not secured the chocks properly.

Shouting then transfers to concern for Miss MacGregor, who regains consciousness with a whimper. The sisters comfort each other. Eventually the injured Miss MacGregor's shin is splinted with stripped matagouri branches and she smiles weakly as she is lifted onto the coach. The uninjured Miss MacGregor pats her hand. 'All better,' she consoles.

'All better, only painful. Bloody painful!' whispers her other half with a giggle that is immediately reciprocated.

With the split shaft strapped tight and the horses refreshed the remaining passengers re-embark. They look at each other in silence.

The wordless boy then ventures an opinion. 'Well, that was a cat-astrophy,' says Robbie Macandrew in a droll tone, looking at Mr Albert Sew Lee. Billie gapes at such an amazingly witty comment and her canted eyes are bright with adoration.

Mr Albert Sew Lee replies in a broad Australian accent. 'Doggone it,' he grins back.

The passengers gasp and start to laugh and slap one another with incredulity.

The nervous tension breaks, thoughts of what could have been a terrible disaster are dismissed, and once again spirits are raised as they recommence their journey. Well behind schedule, they will continue to lag behind this day as Ned nurses the team along to the next staging post at Kyeburn. Peace restored, he breathes deeply of the pungent wild thyme.

The cat yarn is played out with effect for years to come,

and it becomes lore that a giant black panther stalks the Pig-root and sometimes holds up His Majesty's Mail escort so that outlaws may relieve the transport of its cargo.

Eichardt's Private Hotel,
Queenstown, Central Otago.
Wednesday, 25th January, 1871.

Dear Mother Meg and Alf,
    I trust you are well. I am writing to tell you of my safe arrival.
    We had a pleasant journey over two days, trotting along steadily until we arrived at Queenstown. Mr Macandrew ensured I was comfortable and his son Robbie seems satisfactory. I made a new friend Susannah, who travelled with us as far as the Naseby junction. Her parents have bought the Publican's lease to an hotel and they were cheered to know I have lived in licensed premises for many years and am not turned ruffian or disreputable!
    Also in our coach was a Chinaman dressed in fine clothing with a topper hat and sitting up and staring ahead, who did not say a word until we were far along the Pigroot and so we assumed he did not understand our prattling. Then after a long while we found that he knew English very well, as he had been born in Australia and spoke in an educated way! In general, we were a happy group of travellers and our journey was safe. I shall write on Sundays after this, so that you may expect my letters on Tuesdays.
    I trust this finds you both well, as I am.
I remain,
Your loving Ward,
Billie Frost.

CHAPTER
TWENTY-SIX

Central Otago's wild beauty is dazzling. Its colours are strong and its perfumes aromatic. But the region also provides visions that would curdle Meg's blood. From ransacked land left by crazed diggers, to the outcome of those who have become ruined its by excess, there is evidence enough.

The real gold rush, where more than eighteen thousand prospectors scratched away like demons to find 'the colour', has dwindled. After pouring off the ships with their swags, desperate to find gold whatever the cost, most of those men are now either rich, disillusioned or dead. Many of the latter met their end through infection, freezing temperatures or alcohol-induced brawling. Murders by gun, knife and throat-cutting were so common it is said that a man could stumble over half a dozen bodies between the pub and his tent. Some miners preferred the proximity of a few pubs and a grocer. Others isolated themselves further up the rivers. Wherever their placement, their pathetic calico shelters without so much as a ground cloth could not prevent frostbite any more than a diet of mutton and tea could prevent scurvy.

But panning in the rivers has given way to blasting and sluicing for alluvial gold, and cooperatives are employed for wages. Most general stores in trail towns still trade their goods in exchange for gold – there is big money to be made in supplying food, clothing, equipment and lodgings and pubs also keep weighing scales to settle bills. Some miners hold on to their nuggets and chips, though this is a dangerous practice since lawless desperados are always on the lookout for an opportunity to swoop down and relieve them of their earnings.

Times are changing but are still prosperous, especially in the towns, and Queenstown is very much a centre of trade and tourists. The spacious Eichardt's Hotel is positioned adjacent to the glittering Lake Wakatipu. Mayor Bendix Hallenstein has gifted the Queenstown peninsular, on which he formerly ran a sheep station, to the town. Billie surmises that he must be wealthy indeed. She wonders if he might be related to Benny, her school friend of the same surname.

There are many hotels in Queenstown, but in her opinion Eichardt's is the most handsome and is surely superior with its electrical lighting! Across the lake, the Remarkables mountain range juts into the skyline like a cardboard backdrop, too vivid to be real, too real to be fake. The tops are still dusted with snow even though it is high summer.

It is scorching by midday at ground level and Billie flings off her petticoats in the privacy of her room. Without Mother Meg to look askance, she takes herself into the street. No scandal erupts – this is a frontier town where peculiarities are commonplace – and she continues this liberty until dinnertime, when guests dress with the decorum expected at a tourist hotel.

There is little decorum in some other parts of the town. Rats and mice are so plentiful they are fair game; men brag that they kill hundreds in a day's sport. Miners are disagreeably disturbed during their rest by vermin running over their faces and inflicting bites at will, spoiling provisions, gnawing their boots. It is a continuous process to keep the numbers at bay, and exhibitions are a commonplace method of extermination where sacks of rats are released to fight with dogs brought in for the purpose. The standard entry is two shillings and sixpence and the men place bets on the dogs. The one that eliminates the largest number of vermin – usually with swift decapitation – carries the day.

From behind the shed venue, straddling a stack of pallets, Billie watches through a knot-hole in the siding boards. Not permitted to go near gaming rooms and arenas, she easily convinces herself that this time she is merely en route to the foreshore. Initially fascinated with horror, soon she cannot bear the monstrous sport. Repulsed, she turns away and runs towards the lake.

Paddling in the clear, cold water is a grand way to adjust one's senses.

Eichardt's Private Hotel,
Queenstown, Central Otago.
Sunday, 29th January, 1871.

Dear Mother Meg and Alf,
*   I am having a pleasant time, and trust you are having the same.*

*   You will be pleased to know that the food and lodgings are very agreeable here at Eichardt's. When you think of our own big vegetable gardens, you will be amazed to know that the Cook recently paid half a crown for eight potatoes! Mr Macandrew believes that someone is making a fortune on the backs of others. He says that commerce is essential, but greed is not. Without potatoes, Cook often makes scones to have with our meat, as flour is only 5 pence per pound. Yesterday they were flavoured with thyme, which grows wild all around. She says it is also good under the pillow to ward off nightmares. Oh, yes, you can be sure I have inspected the kitchen, as well as all other nooks and crannies, to see what is what!*

*   There is a chandelier in the dining room and I do so love to watch the sun catching the prisms and dancing around the walls.*

*   Robbie is a kind boy and does not patronise me from his position of being three years older. He says that he misses his schooling in one way, but is gaining valuable education in another, and should catch up enough to matriculate in due course from Otago Boys' High. He says he might teach me to play chess.*

There is an abundance of butterflies flitting and fluttering their wings in the sunlight, dear little blue things that swarm around the tussock and the thyme. I shall draw them, but it will not be easy to catch the way they change colours from fawn, to grey, to blue, to violet. Also, there are tiny coppery ones that blend into the landscape so well. This is a glorious place even if much of it looks like a Wild West desert. It is so wide and big, and the light is vibrant and sharp, so different from the soft colours of Dunedin.

I trust little Mungo is well and not missing me too much. I do so miss him!
I remain,
Your loving Ward,
Billie Frost.

CHAPTER
TWENTY-SEVEN

Some days are long and languid, just the thing for reading or dozing. Then, to enjoy the opposite sensation, Billie walks into the lake up to her knees; it is now so familiar and cool. Other days are full of action, like the times when Mr Macandrew takes the young travellers with him on one of his visits to a district bank or gold receiver. 'This is an educational day,' he always begins, 'and I will be pleased to receive your reports in due course. Tomorrow morning will be satisfactory.'

Angus Macandrew's flourishing moustache and abundant eyebrows conceal most of his facial expressions and Billie is not always sure of his intent. Of one thing she is certain: with his dry wit and ready chuckle, Robbie's father is not of the dour breed of Scottish settlers.

This time he hosts the young pair on a journey to Skippers, twenty miles north of Queenstown. As they lurch along the cliff face above the canyon he instructs, 'We're coming up to Hell's Gate – not dynamited, but precisely drilled then filled with water. The frost did the work and the rock cracked. You might think this merely a rough trail, but in fact you will come to see that it is a feat of engineering.'

Billie is not sure she wants to see: they seem to be on the precipice, some three hundred feet above the Shotover River. The river's immense power is manifest. It churns with plumy rapids then races along unimpeded, before slowing to turquoise depths, gentle and deceptive.

'This is the richest river in the world, in my estimation,' Mr Macandrew shouts over the roar. 'Aye, richer than the Klondyke. At this time of year the flow is quite calm, but it surges like a demon in spring when the snows melt. It's been known to rise eleven feet in five hours.'

'Carrying away bridges and strong horses,' intones Robbie, 'according to reports.'

Billie tries to concentrate on the rock formations, rather than imminent death below. She is glad to be on the inner side of the carriage.

'You're not going to be sick, are you?' Robbie grins.

'Never!' responds the bilious girl. 'I just wish to concentrate on the lovely rocks.'

The schist's muted tones calm her anxiety. Flecks of pale yellow pyrite shimmer in the sunlight and the rock face could indeed appear to be elevating. *Fool's gold*, nods Billie, knowing that after scratching in the gravels until they are nearly mad, men have then killed over the worthless mineral.

When the sturdy little mares slow their trot to negotiate some fallen debris she reaches out of the carriage. A gecko, previously motionless in the sun, flicks away under a fissure. The rock is flaky and gravel lies where it crumbles and falls. She lifts a chip as a souvenir, or to study for her report. Then the carriage picks up speed and at a sure-footed pace, they are carried on to Skippers.

It is a lively township, rough and ready like most mining settlements, but with enough to hold the younger guests' interest while Inspector Macandrew carries out his mission at the bank. This culminates in an excellent luncheon at the Otago Hotel and then they are on the homeward stretch. 'One and a half hours in, three hours there, one and a half hours out,' calculates Billie.

'That is,' responds Robbie, 'if we don't fall into the river – oh! *Watch out!*'

Billie screams and lurches away from the apparent danger, before regaining her self-control. It is the first time Robbie Macandrew encounters the Look.

Eichardt's Private Hotel,
Queenstown, Central Otago.
Sunday, 5th February, 1871.

Dear Mother Meg and Alf
I trust you are well. I am having such a splendid time!
Queenstown is just the ticket. There are all number of
people coming and going and I love to watch them. I sometimes
sit and sketch them in my journal, especially the Americans
whose style of dress and manner is quite different than our own.
Madras cotton is the mode and the plaid has peculiar colours
woven side by side, such as orange and blue, or green and purple.
You might imagine that this would look queerly mismatched,
but it is not so. Also, I could not tear my eyes from a most ele-
gant lady dressed fully in cream, only with black trims at the
lapels and cuffs. I do not believe she would wear the same pale
outfit on the streets of Dunedin!
Then I saw a lady with a dress of lavender butterflies on
a yellow background. You know how I love butterflies and I
could not believe my eyes when I saw this fabric, so I approached
the lady and told her of what Robbie calls our 'native Zizina or
common blue'. (If these dear little creatures are 'common', I
would be glad to also be called so!) I am obliged to tell you that I
am not pestering these ladies, as they do call out an invitation to
me.
Instead of wide skirts like ours, theirs are flattened at the
front and swagged up at the back. It sits ever so snug because the

skirt is cunningly cut in shaped gores. They also wear such pretty hats, like little saucers set quite forward on their head. Men also wear bold chequered coats and even yellow trousers! I feel rather drab in comparison, but have been sketching their cloth-ing so ferociously that I soon may require more drawing paper!

I miss Mungo very much, and of course I miss you also. I remain,
Your loving Ward,
Billie Frost.

CHAPTER
TWENTY-EIGHT

Angus Macandrew proposes that Billie join him on the paddle steamer *Antrim* to Glenorchy at the head of the lake; he is conducting business at the Frankton Lodge with William Rees, holder of a huge pastoral empire encompassing much of the Wakatipu basin. During the gold rush the law required grazing to make way for mining if a workable prospect was found. This was a trying time for the family, but due to Mr Rees' enterprising nature they recovered and the farm is again prospering.

From her close position playing draughts with the publican's daughter, Billie listens to what she can about high country runs. But it is fearsome hot inside the crowded public house. She wanders outside and along the gravel foreshore.

The lake is cool and inviting. Its stony bottom feels like satin on her feet – bumpy satin, but so smooth. She wades in with hitched-up skirts, then ties them around her waist. Her chemise can get wet – what harm will it do – and nobody will care a jot. Other bathers are doing similarly and some of the children are almost naked.

How warm is the air and how lovely is the lake's rippling touch. She closes her eyes and – what a marvellous idea! She shall pretend she is Ophelia and lean back on that large bract of driftwood. Here is a twig to represent her flowers: 'There's rosemary, that's for remembrance. Pray you, love, remember. And there's pansies, that's for thoughts,' murmurs Ophelia.

How silky is the water. How tender is its lapping. Her hair trails out and her arms drift with the current. How tranquil she is as the sun embraces her body.

But now – how cold and wet – she is choking and trying to scream and being unable to as the lake pulls at her billowing dress. Ophelia transforms into Billie. She pulls and wrestles and will not be beaten under. Not yet. Not yet.

Yet the pulling is persistent and gentle and persuasive, and she is floating down and down. And soon, all is peaceful.

And now people are splashing and a woman is crying out, and men are carrying her aloft, and they are slapping her back and hanging her upside down. Until a surge of lake spews from her throat and nose and she is coughing now, gasping and gurgling. Coughing from the depths of her being.

Perhaps Billie Frost drowns for a moment in Lake Wakatipu. But now she is all dried out – subdued, chilled. The homeward voyage is restrained and the mountains are stern against the dusky sky.

Eichardt's Private Hotel,
Queenstown, Central Otago.
Sunday, 12th February, 1871.

Dear Mother Meg and Alf,
    I have had another satisfactory week, and trust you have had the same.

    We took a trip up the Wakatipu Lake to Glenorchy with a flock of sheep! Of two-legged passengers we were only six, but lo and behold, also aboard was the American lady with whom I discussed the little blue butterflies! She is on "grand tour" of many months and intends to carry on to the central North Island specially to see the Pink Terraces. She believes them to be the "Eighth Wonder of the World" but I cannot imagine any-thing more wonderful than this lake.

    There was nothing much at Glenorchy except an hotel, but it is where Mr Macandrew met with some men to talk about farming.

    Back in Queenstown, Robbie says that horses are now so plentiful they cannot be sold at a reasonable price and owners prefer to let them run in a paddock, paying two-and-five-pence per week for their accommodation, in preference to selling them at a loss. I suppose this is the best thing to do, although the ground is so very dry. I should not like to be a farmer.

    I am faithfully keeping up my daily journal. I have had a slight chill. I am missing you all very much, but you should not fret as I am now quite well.

Please give Mungo extra hugs from me.
I remain,
Your loving Ward (and Daughter),
Billie.
P.S. The American lady called on me next day and gave me her fashion magazine, called 'Harper's Bazaar'. I thought I should burst from excitement when she said I could keep it!

CHAPTER
TWENTY-NINE

Stars are suspended like a caught breath in the black canopy of night. Billie strains out of her casement window to absorb as much as she can from such an angle. She is bedazzled by the pulsing lights that seem near enough to touch. How marvellous it would be to stroll outside and see more.

She pulls on her mama's shawl and slides along the polished hallway on her bed stockings to the bedroom shared by Robbie and his father. Mr Macandrew is away for two days on business.

'Excuse me, Robbie. I know I shouldn't disturb you in your reading, but I should like to take a walk about outside to look at the stars like the other night. You can test me on the names.'

'Sorry, lassie, no can do. Father told me to keep a strict eye on you and one thing you may not do is go out at night unaccompanied. And you should really not be wandering about in your nightgown, do you think?'

'Bother then. I daresay I can ask Mr Eichardt to find me an escort.'

'I daresay too, that Mr Eichardt is busy in the saloon. Och, don't be a pest, Billie. Just go back to bed now. And remember to lock the door.'

She returns to her room and again leans out of the window to gaze at the heavens. Bother again! She pulls on the clothes that had sufficed during the day and buttons her short boots. No need for petticoats or stockings now. Once again the paisley shawl is slung on and as an afterthought, the tweed cloak that Meg has insisted she bring for travelling and similar situations. Yes, she thinks, it may be rather chilly tonight. But it is not the chill-to-the bone cold of Dunedin, more a crisp shiver.

Most certainly young guests are not permitted in the Public Bar on the ground floor. And they should not be seen in the vicinity at all after 9pm; they must venture no further than the upstairs landing. Eichardt's is a respectable hotel and in a town of much disrespectful behaviour with its gaols full of the consequences, the Proprietor does not encourage any dubious goings on. Billie does not think her plan is dubious; on the contrary, studying the stars is educational, is it not? Who needs an escort? The night is bright with stars and pools of light are flowing from establishments all along the road.

She creeps along the hallway to the rear balcony and deftly negotiates an iron staircase to ground level. She scans the sky, knowing the Southern Cross and Orion's belt, the Milky Way and the brightest light, Jupiter. But they are much more real tonight; she can almost reach out and touch them. Slowly she scuffs along, head upturned, sometimes stumbling on the rutty road, but without concern. When she finally looks ahead, she finds herself far away from Eichardt's. She might as well keep going on, to see what's what.

The route is noisy, filled with grog shops, bars and billiard rooms, punters and revellers. She crosses a paddock into Cow Lane, alive with drunkenness. Men are slumped, or ranting in alcohol-induced fits, or just lying prone in their own vomit. Until they crawl away, or are shoulder-hefted by their companions, likely just as sodden, but still on their feet. Some don't ever make it back to their camps, dying instead of alcohol poisoning, pistol shots or punches to the brain. Life is not all a bed of roses, nor a pan of nuggets, on the goldfields and in the towns – but the brandy and rum and ale flow and the proprietors of their supply get rich on the takings. Billie has seen plenty of drunken individuals over the years and takes it for granted. She does not approve or disapprove, but is only glad that her nearest and dearest are not inclined to be so dissolute.

A ragged dump of hay, placed for the convenience of horses during the daytime, is the perfect place to watch and listen and she curls into it. The sound of entertainment flows out of the many bars and bordellos along the littered lane. Pianos plonky-tonk. Squeezeboxes drone. Harmonicas jag and jaw. Men's rough voices sing, brag, accost. They talk big and squander their makings on bets and booze. They fight over claims or they fight over women. Or they fight simply because there's nothing like a good fight.

A man staggers towards her and belches, then gains focus and leers. 'Whacha doin' here li'l gal? This ain't no place for a li'l gal.' He lears out to grab at Billie's blouse. 'Aw, ya ain't so li'l after all, are ya?!'

She draws back in alarm, suddenly aware of her surroundings, but the drunkard lurches away swigging at his bottle before falling face down in the dust.

Inside the establishments, barmaids serve with come-hither pouts. Pocked crones in gaudy colours cackle, draw on their short pipes and offer their filthy bodies. Younger harlots hitch their bosoms and rock on their men's laps and stroke their egos as they finger the next fool's pocket. Entertainers sing and dance and flutter their satin petticoats while urging the clientele to spend well. Other customers take their cue after little encouragement and are deftly guided upstairs to private apartments.

Billie is cosy in her hay nest, warm and sleepy despite the diabolical cacophony. The noise is deafening – so loud that if anyone screamed nobody would hear.

Nobody does hear the screams of an entertainer in an upstairs room. When her throat is slit and her supple young body is slashed to ribbons. As happens on other occasions, in other goldmine towns.

While gold continues to rattle into the hungry tills.

From the realms of sleep, Billie hears her name being shouted. Someone is shaking her hard. Robbie is hissing, 'You mad lassie – are you a total idiot? I told you to bide inside! And I told you – oh Christ, thank goodness you're all right!'

A group of men is also crowding around, gasping with relief. They have snatched gaslights from Eichardt's front veranda and rushed around the adjacent streets with Master Macandrew, calling and calling her name. Now here she is, half asleep on a hay bale. They are baffled.

'Thank God she's alive. She could have been taken – '

'Whatever possessed her to come here and then sit in a haystack? In the middle of this stink! Is she right in the head?'

'Has she been – ?'

'She looks calm – she looks in order.'

'Jasus, Mary and Joseph, she's stepping down now, cool as you like!'

'If I were her father I'd give her a right walloping, that I would!'

'All right, all right, you blokes,' finalises the leader of the group. 'Let's just give thanks that we've found her. Come on miss, let's carry you back to the hotel.'

Robbie Macandrew can hardly speak for the surge of emotion that overtakes him: anger laced with relief. He knows he will get a fearful drubbing from Father when he finds out. He may even be sent home in disgrace.

'I'm ever so sorry, Robbie,' says Billie earnestly. 'I just

found myself walking under the stars and ended up here. Nothing bad happened and I didn't mean to worry you. I am truly sorry.'

'Don't ever,' he hisses between clenched teeth, 'do anything so bloody daft again.'

Eichardt's Private Hotel,
Queenstown, Central Otago.
Sunday, 19th February, 1871.

My dear Mother Meg and my lovely Alf,

I trust you are both well. I did enjoy reading how Mungo carries your letters in his little mouth as you take them to the Post Office!

The evenings are a tiny bit cold, even though the days are burning hot, as it is rather like a desert, being inland and high up.

Sometimes at night I am wakened by the coaches that arrive late and with much to-do. I look down upon them from above and remember our own journey last month. The stars are so very clear. I can see Orion's Belt and the Southern Cross and the Milky Way. I saw a shooting star flashing across and it was a marvellous sight!

I am learning so much more than I ever knew before, even though some of it is not so pleasant. For example, when I was little and saw the prospectors travelling through Dunedin, wagering on how much gold they were going to find, I felt envious of them. However, as it turned out, in winter many were found in a pitiable state. Their poor feet were frostbitten so badly that some required amputation. Also, many settlements were snowed up without provisions and without any possibility of outsiders reaching them, the snow being over ten feet deep! I am glad I have always been warm enough and although chilblains torture me in winter, I shall try to never complain again.

Mr Macandrew still travels out to do his inspections of the Banks on most weekdays. His territory covers Shotover, Arrowtown, Maori Point, Cromwell, Clyde (which was The Dunstan) and Alexandra districts. He sometimes returns to Queenstown the same day and other times he stays on, then has a few days' rest in between. He must visit Ophir, St Bathans and Naseby before we return.

Tomorrow he is taking me to Arrowtown where we will stay for two days. Robbie will not come this time.

I miss you both and Mungo, but I am in the pink.
I remain,
Your loving Ward and Daughter,
Billie.

CHAPTER THIRTY

———⟋⟍———

Robbie Macandrew distances himself on the pretext of studying. In truth, he is not at all happy playing minder to Billie Frost. She is calamity on legs, in his opinion. Well, not all the time; she is a smart lass and can compete with him on many topics. But at sixteen he really does need to concentrate on his books so he will be up with his classmates when he returns to Boys' High next month. His father is happy to leave him to his own devices if he so wishes.

Angus Macandrew knows the proprietors of the Ballarat Hotel well and is confident his charge will enjoy Arrowtown. Their hosts' son is anticipating Billie's arrival, having heard she is curious and interested in exploring.

Although few Europeans go to the Chinese gardens – they prefer not to mingle with Orientals – young Samuel regularly visits his friend Ah Lum up there and believes his guest will enjoy the outing. It takes the pair forty minutes to negotiate the steep hillside track to his hut. Chinamen are not permitted to dwell within the town boundaries although Ah Lum is respected in the town and serves his Celestial customers without the prejudice often meted out in return.

Nearing his pocket of ground, Billie is amazed to see a profusion of vegetables. In a land of dry tussock and rock, the green abundance spreads in narrow rows right down to the Arrow River below.

The hut is wedged into the cliff, not much more than a pile of rocks precariously stacked and crudely thatched. A feeble fire is set in its core, the smoke drawn outside through a tin pipe. The only other features are a small pallet bed and a few cooking utensils.

Ah Lum beams, but rarely speaks. He rustles into the shadows and brings forth two delicate cups and a twist of tea leaves. He scoops fresh water into a blackened pan and brings it to a rapid boil then places it onto a rock. He sprinkles a few green shreds into the water and waits in silence. Then he pours the steaming liquid with utmost care into one cup, bows to Billie and presents it to her, respecting the strange local custom of serving women first. He repeats the process for Sam. Only then does he pour the brew into his own rough beaker and together they bow. They sip the tea; it is weak but fragrant.

Without much difficulty, through signs and a few words – it is evident he knows more English than he lets on today – Ah Lum confirms that there are many like himself working in the same way around the district. They supply a wide catchment with fruit and vegetables and therefore many think the Chinamen make a considerable profit. But like his countrymen, Ah Lum must pay an increasing poll tax to the government, plus repay his guarantor in China, before he can save even a few pence to bring his wife from China. Ah Lum's eyes dim as he indicates it will be ten years before he sees his bride.

Although the alluvial gravel has given up most of its gold, the Chinese work methodically over the tailings in the wake of the main rushes, satisfied with small returns. Or so the locals believe. But with near-impossible financial straits, some return home penniless. Some succumb to alcohol, or surrender to their opium pipe dreams. A few, like Ah Lum, survive and prosper.

Eichardt's Private Hotel,
Queenstown, Central Otago.
Sunday, 26th February, 1871.

My dear Mother Meg and Alf,
 I trust you are well and Mungo is being a good boy.
 Your last letter did have me laughing over the two
painted ladies in the public bar who turned out to be men.
 This week we were based at Arrowtown, near the middle
of the Province. The town is full of action. The main street is
planted with an avenue of oaks and sycamores, and it is strange
to see English trees in such a setting, but somehow it all fits
together. With autumn approaching, their foliage is starting to
turn, and I daresay the streets will be a mass of golden leaves
before long.
 I visited one of the local Chinese gardeners, whose fruit
and vegetables are supplied far and wide. To tend his garden,
even without rain, he carries buckets of river water up the hill-
side several times a day. What gumption! He wears his head
shaven except for a long braid, but he is a very nice man. His
face is happy, but I noticed such sad eyes. As we said farewell he
presented me with a small celadon tile. It is like a pale green
coin, and he indicated this will bring me luck! I shall treasure it
and always remember his kindness.
 Soon we shall be homeward bound, the last stop being
Naseby where I do so hope to meet my friend Susannah once
again! Mr Macandrew is not so sure that this can be achieved.

I miss you very much, even more than last week.
Your very loving Daughter,
Billie.

The Royal Hotel,
Naseby, Central Otago.
Wednesday, 1st March, 1871.

Dearest Mother Meg and Father Alf,
    You will get a surprise to receive this letter so soon after the last, but I assure you all is well and I am now at Naseby!
    You will also get another surprise to know that we shall be arriving home in a few days' time, instead of the end of next week! Mr Macandrew's work will finish on Friday and so we shall leave the following morning. It will be such a thrill to see you, so I shall write just a little more because I shall surely forget it in the excitement of seeing you and Mungo!
    You will not guess where we are to stay for three days and nights? It is at the Royal Hotel, which is run by Susannah's parents! Mr Macandrew had been very gloomy to me about my seeing Susie, saying that it was a large town and that he did not intend to dally. But he had been jesting all along, as he planned that we should stay here!
    Indeed, Naseby is not large at all, but a small town. Oh, it is so thrilling to see my friend once more. We two have quickly become bosom buddies. Please have no fear at my language, as Susie says it is American and she learned it from a reliable coach driver who is from Texas.
    We had such an agreeable time and Susie also plays chess. I did not play, as I had come to realise before now that I am a real duffer at the game. She played with Robbie, whom I

believed would take her easily. But in the event, she captured his King! It was a fine challenge, although I still cannot see how one understands the strategy and manoeuvres – and I doubt I ever shall. My brain is not made that way, and that is that.

Yesterday Robbie gave me a small gold nugget. It is about the size of a half-pea. He purchased it from a boy his own age who was offering it for sale as we walked along the street. Most gold is traded to the bank agent, but in this case Robbie gave two pounds to the boy who was trading it. Two pounds! Then when he presented it to me I could not believe my eyes! He said it was a token of our educational tour of the goldfields. Robbie is a rather quiet boy but very droll, and I assume he inherits that from his Father. We have become good friends, although I suppose that when he returns to his chums at Boys' High he may not see it that way. He plans to go to the University after he matriculates, to read Political Economy. It sounds very dull, but Robbie says it is about production and trade and he expects to enjoy it.

I shall be home on Saturday night, almost before you receive this, my last letter. I cannot imagine how five weeks have gone by with such speed! How I look forward to seeing your faces, and to hug you so tightly.
Your very loving and excited Daughter,
Billie.

CHAPTER
THIRTY-ONE

Saturday's homeward journey starts quietly enough. Invigorated by the last few days' hospitality and wrapped against the warning press of autumn, they board the Cobb & Co stagecoach. They are sad to leave such bonhomie, but very glad to be nearing their loved ones after such an absence.

The whip bows ostentatiously as he assists the ladies into the coach. 'Cabbage Tree Ned!' Billie is ecstatic. 'Gidday again!' Their driver could have been one of a dozen now plying the route, but as circumstance would have it, here is the one and only Ned Devine.

'Bugger me days!' he laughs. 'You have shot up, young lady – shot up tall since I last had the pleasure! I wager we shall have a trouble-free journey this time, hey? No wild cats this time hey what!'

He orders the lead pair to perform their showy rear-up before they settle into a brisk trot along the Naseby Road.

Being a public coach and not a gold transport escorted by a team carrying carbines and revolvers, there is no hint of trouble.

Until they near the Pigroot junction. Suddenly, from out of a tussock bluff, comes an uproar of shouting and gunfire. Armed bandits descend upon the coach and challenge its driver and occupants: 'Stand and deliver!'

Passengers scream, leathers screech, horses rear, and pandemonium sets in over a half-minute that seems like many.

Angus Macandrew takes control. 'Wheesht, all of ye, and listen to me now! Dinna move. Turn out your pockets and reticules. Toss your coins and trinkets onto the ground. Do *not* show any fear. Sit tight and do *not* look about.' And as the agitation subsides he adds, 'Stay calm ladies, and keep seated gentlemen. Equanimity is the best form of defence.'

Billie is agog with the thrill of it – 'Stand and deliver!' To think she should hear those words right out of the Wild West of America. But when Ned Devine swears violent, bloodthirsty oaths at these outlaws and the terrified horses scream, her body reacts with bolts of fright.

However, Devine knows this band of robbers; he knows the blighters are aware there's unlikely to be loot on this stage. They are just posturing and enjoying themselves. 'You bloody bastards! Hell's bells – just look what's been done to me brake straps! Ripped to smithereens by the pressure and me horses practically frothing with fright. You know there ain't no gold on this transport! Piss off and don't let me see your bloody arses again!'

And as the wild men whirl their mounts and gallop back into the hills shooting at the sky and laughing hilariously, he thunders after them, 'You'll be too big for your britches one day, mateys!'

Ned comforts his passengers, all of them still shaking. 'You behaved like troopers and that's a fact. I salute you in staying calm. Here's a tot of brandy to calm your nerves – yes, even you should take a swig, missie. Now folks, at least no harm has come of it, so we'll be on our way as soon as we fix the bloomin' brake leathers.' His handsome grin and assured stance belies his fury, and by the devil, if any other coachman dares to mock him for the incident he'll flatten him!

Other horsemen have galloped ahead and by the time the coach draws in to Wain's Hotel, news of the stickup has arrived. There is Meg, weeping at the thought of her darling being shot up. There is Alf, beaming with relief. Hugging and kissing and more hugging and more tears.

Billie knows her tiny gold nugget and celadon tile are still safe in the seam of her petticoat. She also knows it will be impossible to conceal the bandit situation from her guardians. The 'holdup without a cause' will become front page news.

PART THREE

CHAPTER THIRTY-TWO

Otago Girls' High School has not had many settling-in issues and Billie starts on the first day of its second term. The scratchy serge skirt is annoying after the freedom of summer cotton. Starting directly into fourth form on the basis of her application results, she is introduced to a range of new subjects. Greek is difficult because she has missed the basics, but it is becoming more enjoyable. English and history are what she continues to favour best, followed by Latin and botany. But she is a duffer at dancing, hopeless at calisthenics and worse at music. Drawing lessons sounded fun, but she must only sketch flowers in vases this year, so very dull.

She makes friends and enjoys her study, but it isn't easy to be orderly. There are not the escapades she had hoped for. It may not be a private college teaching girls how to become ladies, but it still maintains very strict discipline.

Under the firm hand of Lady Principal, Mrs Margaret Burn, there is certainly no kicking about. The two classrooms are housed in a two-roomed wing of Boys' High; Mrs Burn takes some lessons and masters from the boys' school take others under the strict eyes of lady chaperones. A fence has been built between the designated areas to guard against the perceived threat of marauding boys. The notion has exercised many a parent and it is an excellent topic of conversation at dinner, especially now that a girl had been caught trying to jump high enough to peep over. Billie is disinterested in the fence, soon to become even higher; she has other things to keep her mind active.

As agreed between Mr Northey and the school board, she is permitted to attend only four days a week and to assist Mr Ogilvy on Wednesdays. The prospect of continuing her cadetship is very satisfactory, especially now that she is paid one shilling for the day. At three-thirty on Tuesdays she hurtles down View Street and steadies herself into Moray Place, where she straightens her blouse and skirt before walking smartly to the rooms of Ogilvy and Ogilvy, Barristers & Solicitors. There she receives instructions for the next day; this is at Billie's request – she does not wish to spend precious time on Wednesdays being briefed on the day's work. James Ogilvy holds in his amusement as he outlines her duties.

Some tasks are to run documents hither and thither across town, while others are to concentrate on mundane but essential details of office presentation. She continues to accompany her employer to the Law Courts in Lower Stuart Street in the early afternoon.

Some cases interest her and some repel her sensibilities. The Look crosses her face as she ponders some scenarios. Mr Ogilvy says he must try that in court.

James' colleagues doff their hats with a smile as they pass the odd couple making their way into the court building. Upon arrival, Billie occupies herself in the foyer until the end of the session, sketching its architectural features or staring deep into the golden kauri timber with its shimmering grain and subtly changing hues. Sometimes she is permitted to watch proceedings from the public gallery and enjoys these just as much. She also watches the intense scribbling of the court reporter, whose florid accounts in the next day's *Times* often bear little resemblance to the mundane proceedings.

Much is humdrum – bankruptcies, common assaults, thievery and civil litigations – although James is becoming increasingly interested in the land confiscation issues and hopes to study the Native Land Act in the near future.

Meanwhile, he instructs her that his representations in court are based not on emotions but on points of law and its interpretation. James is not the most erudite barrister, but his skills lie in reducing cases to their essentials and exposing the basic principles of common law. His presentations are clear and focused and he maintains exquisite politeness which makes him popular at the Bar.

Billie can see that his courtesy and doggedness often helps him win his case in the end.

CHAPTER
THIRTY-THREE

December 1871

These days, Edwin is struggling with the sense of it all. As he walks from his tailor, having been fitted for two new suits made from fine local Roslyn worsted wool, he is in a quandary. Why, he asks himself, does he persist in spending so much energy on a girl who is not his responsibility?

He has continued to write to Alton regarding family matters and, just as systematically, Alton has chosen to ignore these advances, writing back instead of society matters, the ball he is hosting and other such absurd extravagances. Balls – at Thornbury! It may sound a grand manor, but it is in fact a modest estate. Has the fool ripped open the walls of the drawing room? Quarterly reports seem to be in order, but although Alton's allowance is generous, how is he paying for such lavish functions? It is disturbing, and now that Alton has failed to communicate for many months, Edwin is concerned about the family estate as well as Billie Frost's future.

Oh, God, why is it all closing in on him? Edwin can only suppose that he feels the burden of filial responsibility since his father's recent death, being the eldest of his five siblings. He wrestles with the issue over and over and then, during periods of ease, assures himself that he is behaving normally in playing the covert role of uncle until proven otherwise. Well, at least established. Damn that bally Alton and his arrogance in sending no reply to his latest series of letters. He consults his best friend and counsel once more.

'My dear fellow,' sighs James Ogilvy, 'you cannot disguise the facts: you are at best a genuine benefactor and at worst mulish slave with no authentic information. I wager I've never witnessed such devotion to righting a perceived wrong. In my opinion your involvement, although exemplary, has coloured your logic significantly.

'So, Eddie, my thoughts are these: with your excellent father having passed away, and your inheritance being not only his considerable holdings here in New Zealand, but his estate at Home, why not make a journey back there? It might serve to clear your mind of this continuous anxiety. To look over the estate and ensure its management is all in hand could be a real tonic.'

Edwin nods, still brooding – but a light starts to glimmer in his mind.

James continues, 'Indeed, it will give you an opportunity

to confront your brother in person, rather than to leave it to constant correspondence which seems to get you nowhere. I daresay Alton is a cad and a bounder in many respects, but probably not such a bad chap. He may be overseeing your estate properly; if not, you shall be in a better position to see for yourself and ensure everything is being dealt with correctly. I suspect all you want is to have Alton's acknowledgement of likely paternity, but I would suggest the likelihood of this, or any voluntary compensation, is slim.

'In any case, Eddie, you need clarity of mind, rather than dithering from year to year. Either decide on a future strategy or put the matter to rest. Then I feel you should be able to proceed with your marriage to your fiancée without burdensome thoughts. What do you say?'

Edwin acknowledges he has indeed been suffering from the effects of his father's sudden death. He feels guilty at not attending on Amy Barnes as well as he might, considering they are engaged. She is the sweetest girl, an old family friend as these things often go, and she will be a perfect wife. He has been going around in circles for far too long and must change direction.

'You are right, James; you are right indeed. It is time I stopped fussing and dithering. Poor Amy has made reference to my absentmindedness on several occasions and I must say I have been feeling unworthy of her recently. She will come to live at Elm Row after we marry; my mother is attending to redecorating our wing to help her through mourning. We shall set a date soon, and by the time I return, I'll have hopefully clarified matters with my brother. Or at least,' he laughs, 'ensured Thornbury hasn't gone to the dogs!'

'So – ostensibly a passage to England to inspect the estate?' asks James.

'A capital idea. I'll book a passage directly and – I do believe I am starting to feel more clear-headed already!'

'Upon my soul, Eddie, it only needed talking through. Something we men are not so good at on a personal level, I believe!' James smiles wryly.

'Indeed. And there is something else I shall talk through with you soon,' Edwin rushes on, as if a dammed creek has burst its banks. 'Yes, something else that must be given serious consideration.'

CHAPTER
THIRTY-FOUR

It is a few days into the New Year and the Maguires have invited Edwin to toast it. More correctly, Edwin has hinted that he would like to visit under the guise of the same. Meg and Alf know his tactics and are happy to have him call upon them.

Alf wears his new three-piece suit despite the warm weather. It is from Bing, Harris & Co quality outfitters, and is his first for many years, made possible by Billie's regular contributions. At precisely two o'clock he ushers Edwin onto the wide front veranda, settles him with Meg and carries out a tray of lager and fruit cake. Mungo is, as ever, in attendance when cake crumbs are possible.

They talk about the brilliance of the weather, the clarity of the beer and a range of summer-day trivia. Then Edwin clears his throat. 'I shall be leaving shortly for England to conduct some business on behalf of my – ' Edwin falters.

'My late father has left affairs that I need to attend to at Home. Listen to me – "at Home"! My home is certain here in New Zealand!'

Meg and Alf wait, as usual, for the real reason to emerge.

'That is to say: I just wished to inform you that things will be the same as before whilst I am away – and I am certain to be back by August. Meanwhile, I just wish you to know that Mr James Ogilvy is taking care of my affairs and that he is your man to call upon if there are any issues with Billie. Which, of course, there will not be! But it is my wish, nevertheless, to let you know that I have secured a last-minute passage and am due to leave next week.'

The Maguires transmit to each other, *Mercy, is that all this is about? We thought it might be something serious!*

'Then let's toast your safe journey, Mr Northey, sir.' Alf removes his jacket, now more casual for the purpose of supping beer and consuming cake.

Edwin departs for England on the iron barque HMS *May Queen* and life goes on in Maclaggan Street.

Billie continues with her schooling and the weekly cadet programme; continues to dance down the street; continues to stumble when she looks upwards at the extensive developments of buildings rising from the earth. Bell Hill has finally been smoothed away and Princes Street flows clearly through to George Street, and Stuart Street is less impeded between its upper and lower parts. A grand new version of First Church is being built in Dowling Street on the hill's stump and is purported to become a most stunning attribute to Dunedin and the glorification of God. Mr Ogilvy says it will look like the Norman cathedrals of England and will have a spire reaching over one hundred and eighty feet skywards.

On Friday afternoons Billie makes a point of looking out for Robbie Macandrew on the corner of Stuart and Castle Streets as he pedals his bone-shaking velocipede home for the weekend. How grand he looks, up high on that contraption. She wants one too! Although a female cyclist would be howled at, she doesn't care. 'One day I shall ride a bicycle,' she tells herself.

Robbie rides by with his friends and doffs his hat if he sees her. Billie is sensitive enough to know that she should not call out to him at these times. On other occasions when he is alone, he stops for a chat, saying that he is overwhelmed by his studies at university but is enjoying them nevertheless. He listens gravely to her contributions to the conversation; she knows his mind is on other more important things and she must not blather. On the farewell he always shakes her hand and says with that wry grin, 'A pleasure, Miss Frost,' before re-mounting his transport for the long ride down the Portobello road.

An errand takes Billie to lower Rattray Street, where she once hustled for a coin. Carriage boys still come and go and or two of her peers have done well for themselves. She knows Tama has become a fisherman, Tommy has become a train guard and Harold is learning a trade at the woollen mills – but it is said that some are now in trouble with the law or worse. Life-on-the-chance sorts the men from the boys.

She recalls her gratitude to Tinks for taking her on those seven years before and knowing that, by the time she left, she was masquerading as a boy.

And here he is, still overseeing affairs after all this time!

'Tinks, how do you do! How are you these days? Time has rushed along, has it not? But I was just thinking, I never did take the opportunity to thank you properly. You stood up for me and I wanted to say how I appreciated your – your patronage.'

He draws deeply on a small stub of tobacco and leers. Billie has been in his sights since her arrival back at Maclaggan Street. 'Look at ye, Bill, bustin' outa yer bodice! Quite a sight, now ye've developed. Anyhows, I t'ought you'd be back one day to see me.'

'Tinks, I only wanted the opportunity to – '

'Well, I knew it would come to a partin' of da ways evench-ly. And I heard you went up Central last year. I was t'inkin' of going up that dat way meself, but I have me boyos to see to – ' he preens.

'If you do go, you'll find it exciting and different and there are great chances up Central. I wager you'd really enjoy it,' replies Billie. 'But now that we've met up again, I want to say how I appreciate the chance of learning how to get along and make a bob or two in these parts. And the fact you took me on as a little 'un.'

'To be sure, Bill, I took ye on cos I knowed you was different, not dat I made any advance on da situation at da time. But look at ye now.' A lizardly flick moistens Tinks's lips.

'Thank you, Tinks, I do appreciate – '

'Appreciate, me arse. Sure you do, little Bill. Just one t'ing – '

'Yes?'

'I knowed ye's a girl all along, right from da start. Not because ye had me fooled, cos ye didn't. I took ye on cos ye had bollocks. But ye're on to better t'ings dese days, as I predicted to meself. Good luck, so,' Tinks says magnanimously.

'Thank you kindly.' Billie offers a friendly handshake, but his eyes have a strange glitter, an unnerving gleam that is dark and dangerous. His grip lingers and he says in a cracked voice, half-boy, half-man, 'Sure, I'll bed ye one day, I will!'

Billie shies back and a chill runs through her. 'Wed?' She laughs uncomfortably. 'What tosh! I assure you, I shan't be wed until I'm old!'

'I'm not talkin' about weddin' ye, darlin'. I'm talkin' about somet'in' else entirely. Come on, I knows ye want it.'

'Want – what?'

'Yer nose is flat like ye run into a wall, an' yer eyes are queer yella, but somehow ye're gorgeous, a glow about ye dat intrigues me,' Tinks oils. 'An' ye came to find me, sure ye did. Ye came to me like I knowed you would. Come on, Bill, let's be havin' ye. Let's be doin' it!' Usually as delicate as a cat teasing a mouse, Tinks now becomes clumsy. He grasps at her budding breast with one claw and her buttocks with the other.

'What?! Are you mad? Get off – stop grabbing at me! Unhand me! Stop it, I say, you vile brute!'

Billie spins away in disbelief, her eyes blazing. Tinks Toomey flinches too, damns himself, then swiftly resumes his usual swagger and calls after her in a strangled croak, 'Ye ninny, I'm only after jokin' ye!'

CHAPTER
THIRTY-FIVE

Thornbury
West Yorkshire
England
Thursday, 30th May 1872

My dear Ogilvy

I have booked my passage back on the 'Inglewood', due to sail from London on 23rd June. She is a smart barque and – while not the speediest of vessels – is under the command of a fine Yorkshire man, so we shall be in safe hands! Arrival is estimated at Port Chalmers on 19th September. By Jove, I expected to be away much longer, but by God's grace and fair weather, I shall be joining you at the Club in the near future.

As you know, when I arrived here, my immediate job was

to find my brother Alton, but that was easier said than done.
My other priority was to visit Thornbury and check on its
management. And as you know from my earlier dispatch, I was
utterly appalled at its condition. The manor house was in a
shambles and the farm was going to the dogs and so, once I had
installed myself, I set about the business of addressing the situation.

My quest was then, in conjunction with this unpleasant
revelation, to find my brother and hold him to account. What I
found out will not make pretty reading, my friend. It transpired
that the blackguard has not only succumbed to many vices, but
has racked up substantial debt on the estate. In a nutshell, that
is it. Yet I feel the need to let you have more detail so here it is:

I have always known my brother to be weak and so after
my anger -- and yes, fury -- had subsided somewhat, I knew I had
to take myself under control and find him, for what good would
it do me to come all this way to lose my senses and not achieve a
result?

He had not replied to letters sent variously to Thornbury,
to his Club in Leeds, and to other establishments I thought he
might frequent. I put a colleague onto it and it wasn't too long
before one of his men tracked him down, in London if you please.
He was in a very bad way, although he still dresses like a toff,
frequenting one Club after the next. Each time I met with him,
he would insist on taking me to a fine hotel for luncheon. There,
after a nip or three, he would become humble and beseech me to
forgive him, then consume more brandy before stumbling off,

leaving me to foot the bill, of course. I was able to see through his game but went along with it for a few times, in the hopes that I could help him out of Queer Street. It was not to be. When I broached the subject of a possible connection to a young lady back in 'fifty-eight, he would hear nothing of it and offered to punch me for the suggestion. He also would not hear of my admonitions regarding Thornbury, claiming it was his to do as he pleased, since Father sent him Home. This is, of course, not the case. Our final luncheon ended in an unseemly way due to his intoxication and raving. I tell you, it was hellish to witness such disagreeable behaviour.

Previous to my ending it, I accompanied him to his favourite haunts - that is, those that still would accept him onto the premises. There were 'ladies' by his side frequently, so nothing has changed in that direction. His companions seem either to be keen to take on his bid, or to challenge him to a duel over debts. I do not hold out much hope for any of his wastrel crowd, who take opium and engage in other despicable habits. It is a wretched situation indeed, but I have done my best for my brother and can do no more.

Now, onto the estate at Thornbury that Alton was 'managing' after the lease had ended. Despite the reports that all was in order, and the Books that indicated the same, this was not the case. He had put a married couple into the House as overseers, but due to the fact they had not been paid regularly for some time, they had no enthusiasm in keeping the place in good order, nor in overseeing the maintenance, as no tradesman could be engaged due to bad debts. Yes, I hear you saying, 'What in Damnation were the lawyers doing?' More of that directly.

Then there is the farm itself. Our tenant farmers were doing the best they could, but they were afraid out of their wits that I was there to demand a higher lease, as apparently my brother had threatened this from time to time. As to the animals, they were in good shape due to the tenants' husbandry, but other maintenance had gone downhill due to the lack of capital input for the last few years.

I was shocked and sickened beyond belief to know that those whom my Father and his Father before him had employed and housed, were left in this situation. It grieved me, too, as I had known these good people all my life. I made haste in righting as much of the wrong as I could.

It was then that another appalling fact came to light. The Law Firm whom my family have been with for generations has been derelict in its duty in the extreme, due to the Senior Partner having departed this earth, and a Junior Partner having taken over the administration of Thornbury. This would have been satisfactory, had he himself not been a swindler! It transpires that he also has the same tastes as Alton Northey, Esquire, and being an old school chum, was charmed by Alton into advancing him continuous funds. Not only that, it appears this scoundrel was taking a substantial commission of his own, by cleverly administering the situation so that discrepancies were not obvious. The accounts that were mailed quarterly to New Zealand always appeared to be in order and I daresay if I hadn't come Home to check on affairs, the situation could have gone on until Doomsday. I am glad to report that this scurrilous individual has been relieved of his post and is now enjoying time at Her Majesty's Pleasure.

As it stands, over some six years Alton has sucked the estate to a low ebb through his addictions to vice or in paying off debts of his own. I am so very glad that Father did not live to know of this awful situation, for they loved the estate and Mother was fierce sad to leave. One excellent fact remains, and that is that all other financial investments are sound and very profitable.

So that is that, and I shall now look to the future. Everything is paid up, tenants are happy and most importantly, my brother has no access to anything other than the stipend I have allocated for him. I am in the process of appointing a new manager to run the entire estate and working hard at concluding all that must be done before June.

So, my dear fellow, I shall soon be aboard the 'Inglewood', and shall see you some twelve weeks after that. Perhaps you might tell our young Miss Frost that I shall also be happy to see her?

I remain,
Yours faithfully,
Edwin J. Northey

CHAPTER
THIRTY-SIX

11th September 1872

Billie flexes her toes inside her woollen stockings and stout boots as she marches towards Ogilvys. She has itchy chilblains, brought on by wearing lighter shoes last week; it is technically spring but the earth has not yet thawed. 'Feckin' freezing' or 'soddin' sodden,' Alf used to call the chilling conditions before his loving voice became mute.

It is not that Billie is consciously vain, but she loves wearing fetching clothes, and the Prussian blue kid boots do so match the gloves she has dyed with ink. They also go well with her moss-green jacket – 'blue and green should never be seen' does not concern Billie Frost. Mrs Ivimey still loves sewing and with Tempe her only living child to accommodate, takes pleasure in fashioning garments for her

245

daughter's friend. Billie still visits Ben Solomon's treasure trove and barters for items that she visualises can be reconfigured. A leather bootlace can be threaded through a hatband. A key can be crimped and fashioned into a brooch. Worn leather gloves can take on new life by trimming the fingers and edging them with braid. And of course, dyes can turn an old outfit into a fashionable statement.

But, as with the wearing of kid boots in September, pride has its just reward and Billie's toes itch and throb. She is glad to reach the doorway of Ogilvys, and stamps loudly up the stairs, one more trick for circulation. Mr Ogilvy Senior does not arrive these days before eleven so she is safe and Mr James does not mind a little clatter. When she finds his door ajar she is surprised. The door has its signals: fully open is for interaction and closed is for no disturbance. Ajar is not the normal procedure.

She peers obliquely into his office. 'Good morning, Mr Ogilvy,' she says then draws back. But James Ogilvy calls to her. 'Come in, my dear, come in directly and shut the door.'

His face is ashen. His hands are trembling. He is standing – Mr James never stands when Billie enters. He is sucking on his pipe and his chest is heaving. Whatever is wrong with him? Oh, whatever has she done to make him so upset?

'Miss Frost, I have some bad news. Sit down, sit down.'

Never has she sat on a chair in this office and she cannot do it now.

'Very well,' he concedes, 'but it is bad news, bad news indeed. How to put it? My dear child, I have no other way of saying this to you: it is our dear friend, Mr Edwin Northey.

He has – has been taken from us. I have to tell you – he is dead.'

The floor is parting and endeavouring to swallow her up. The ceiling is swimming towards her. She slumps forward onto the floor boards. James moves shakily from behind his desk and is grateful that she is already picking herself up.

'You must sit down, Miss Frost. There. Yes, it is true; I am so very grieved to say, it is true. He was safely aboard at Gravesend on the 27th of May, safely aboard and in good health. Then – ' James fights for control of his voice. 'I – we – received a cable yesterday. A cable that Eddie, that is our beloved Mr Northey, had been taken – '

James is quivering, and Billie is gasping.

He manages to continue. 'He had been taken ill. Very ill indeed, caught the typhoid and – and despite everything being done that could be done, and his very strong consti-tution – dear me – ' he inhales deeply. 'Yes, despite all, our friend gave up the ghost – and only a week out of his sched-uled arrival back at Port Chalmers. Oh my dear girl!'

Billie sits rigid in the studded leather chair. 'No, please do not say this, please do not say that Mr Northey is not coming back! Please do not say that my lovely Mr Northey has died! Please, oh please, tell me this is not true!'

'I have much regret in confirming that this is the case, and my sincere condolences to you. You will see that I am very indisposed about this too and do not wish to believe it true. But it has been confirmed so, and his soul has been committed to our Lord, and his body – to the deep.' He draws in a ragged breath.

Billie pitches up at his chest. He aware of the impropriety but is in no way able to desist and they cling to each other.

James then draws himself back and takes in several breaths. 'And therefore, Miss – Billie my dear, I must ask that your guardians come to this office at their earliest convenience, so that I may speak with them.'

Their convenience is two days later; Meg cannot just absent herself from the kitchen. She and Alf now perch on the stiff office chairs and look about the room lined with dark leather tomes. She cannot imagine how Billie endures such an environment, although no doubt she is not just stuck in this office, but running errands elsewhere.

Mr James Ogilvy is now speaking. 'My dear Mr and Mrs Maguire, it is my difficult duty to administer the will of Mr Edwin Northey.' He pauses while Meg struggles to control her spilling eyes. 'It is usual for all the interested parties to be called together for this occasion, but not today. It has been decided – that is, I did not wish to bring Miss Billie into the picture quite yet. But please don't be alarmed. My purpose here today is to advise you that Mr Edwin Northey – ' he inhales deeply ' – having inherited his late father's estate, which includes his Dunedin homestead and a substantial amount of other interests, did revise his situation before his departure last summer.'

The Maguires are still perplexed.

'Therefore, upon his tragic death, I am in the process of executing the above-mentioned will. I shall not go into details that do not concern you in the matter, only what does concern you. It is my duty today to advise you, Mr and Mrs Maguire, that you are to be bequeathed five thousand pounds, with the recommendation that you might purchase a property in your own name.'

Meg is without speech. Alf shakes his head slowly. The room is silent, and as sunlight strikes dust motes that drift within the whirls of cigar smoke, they seek each other's hands. This is surely nonsense – they must have heard wrong. Twice they beg Mr Ogilvy to repeat himself. It takes some time for his words to penetrate. Five thousand pounds is a fortune – my Lord, it is ten times the value of their dear little home that burned to the ground. It is surely more like the cost of a large property on the Rise!

Meg finally finds her voice. 'Five thousand pounds? Oh, my heavens, whatever for? Perhaps it is to be divided in three, against Alf, myself and Billie? But whatever would we do with such an amount? Of course we might buy a cottage but why – ?'

'Mrs Maguire, there is no stipulation for you to buy a property if you do not wish. There is no stipulation at all, only the suggestion that you might wish to settle down in your own home at some future time. Also, there are no instructions for the bequest to be divided into three.'

'Pinch me, Alf – I must be having a dream!' whispers

Meg. 'I cannot comprehend this – only that if I wake and it is not a dream – '

Billie, they silently agree with their eyes.

'It is on behalf of Billie, is it not?' Meg offers and Alf nods. 'And we shall indeed be grateful that we can provide for her into the future!'

'Billie,' states James Ogilvy, 'does not feature in this equation.'

The Maguires cannot take it in. On the one hand, Mr Edwin Northey has decided to bequeath them an enormous amount of money. On the other hand, it is evidently not to be used for Billie. They do not understand.

'No, my dear Mr and Mrs Maguire, your ward is to inherit in her own right. According to the dictates of the will, Miss Billie Frost is, in the first instance, to retain the scholarship funds for her continuing education. And in the second instance, she will have access to another inheritance when she turns twenty years of age.'

'Turns twenty? Access to an inheritance?' Meg is further confounded.

'Indeed, turns twenty. The first of September 1858 was established to be the day of her birth. Therefore, on the first of September 1878 when she reaches her majority, Miss Frost will inherit investments to the sum of fifty thousand pounds.'

CHAPTER
THIRTY-SEVEN

April 1873

Billie tries to focus on her school studies They are in danger of boring her to death these days; it is only the challenge of a correct answer that drives her. Thank goodness she will finish sixth form at the end of the year and leave Girls' High. Most lessons are easy and she tries to look interested while the teacher taps at the blackboard. She can comprehend well ahead of the instruction and has marked time so often that she has recently been advanced to the upper form despite being two years younger than most students. She could go on to university to study something more challenging, but she isn't a boy so that isn't possible. Perhaps she could be a student teacher for Miss Clayton, which she can do when she turns sixteen, although that doesn't really appeal much.

She trudges up the hill to school without engagement, and later scuffs slowly to Ogilvys. She is often quite out of temper. She regains better spirits, then a clutch of sadness envelops her and she fights an acute sense of loss.

So many months after Mr Northey's death, it all seems surreal. He has left her a continuing education plan, but the excitement of education has waned. She just wants his dear self to return. Mr Edwin is – was – not family as such, but was such a familiar figure these past six years. He is – was – like an uncle to her.

Tonight she is reading quietly in her corner of the Abbeyleix kitchen, warm and cosy with good illumination from the paraffin lamps. Autumn's sting has set in, so kitchen reading is her regular enjoyment of an evening. She stretches and decides to sing, as she did when she lay with Mungo beside Mama. She loves the swooping melody of *The Gypsy Girl's Dream* and her husky voice begins:

> *I dreamt I dwelt in marble halls*
> *With vassals and serfs at my side –*

How silly!

> *And of all who assembled within those walls*
> *That I was the hope and the pride.*

I had riches all too great to count, could boast
Of a high ancestral name –

'Sillier still,' she sighs, but continues at random, caressing the lilting notes in her off-key way.

I dreamed that ... knights upon bended knee ...
... pledged their faith to me ...
I also dreamed which charmed me most,
That you lov'd me still the same,
That you lov'd me ...

She just cannot concentrate on her reading. Her drawing tablet and basket of trims might be the thing. She still loves fabric and textiles and can draw fashions by the hour. This atones for her bumbling sewing and skew-whiff prototypes that Mrs Ivimey transforms like magic.

She is happier now, immersed in the feel of a small strip of fur – how soft and warm it is, how comforting.

But I also dreamed –

A loud rapping brings Billie back to her senses. She opens the kitchen door to Robbie Macandrew. He has recently left his Portobello home to be closer to the university and has digs in northern Castle Street. He is tall and lean, the quiet boy having given way to the assured authority of a young man.

'What are you doing skulking around out there, Mr Macandrew? Roamin' in the gloamin'?'

'Lassie, the Lights – they're playing up the sky tonight!'

'Yes, I have heard as much, and beautiful by all accounts.'

'And I have come – well, I was nearby – and here I am to show you them!'

'Mister Macandrew, you cool liar – "nearby" phooey! It is a good half hour's walk from the varsity.' Billie turns away and pinches her cheeks for a little colour.

'So what? I happened to be halfway – all right then, I just thought I should come and discuss them with you, after an absence of two years, and now they are playing! The magical Aurora Australis awaits your inspection!'

Billie sulks. 'But I can see the glow from here. And it's not magic as well you know – it's just a magnetic force disturbed by solar wind.'

'Pardon me, what a spoilsport! I've come all this way – but I did so want to share the Lights with you Frostie, and I know you enjoy staring at the night sky! Come on, you can see it so much better further up and I promise you it will be superb. Or – ' he pulls an exaggeratedly sad face '– shall we just stop here and play a boring game of dominos?'

'Don't mind what I do.'

'Well, well. I don't believe I've seen you without gumption. I've not seen that defeatist attitude in you before.'

'Defeatist – never!' retaliates Billie. 'All right, you monster, you shall not win, even if you think you have! I'll come!'

Billie knows her behaviour is mischievous. When did she start to pout, and show off, and toss her hair? Why is she pretending to hitch up her stocking at this moment? After a little more posturing as she wraps up for the cold, they both head out onto the street. 'Brrr, it's so braw!' she shivers and Robbie mocks himself: 'Aye, a braw bricht moonit nich t'nich! So let's get wurum by spruntin' up yon brae to get a better leuk.'

'No, no, let's just – '

'Och, dinna fesh, womun! No – ' he reverts to his flattened dialect '– the street around here is awash with the dregs. Not you, Frostie, just the clientele! Come on, let's climb on past the muck and slesh and see the Lights more clearly further up! That's the spirit, lassie,' smiles Robbie as he adjusts her thick tweed cloak.

'And please,' he pleads as Billie executes a clumsy whirl, 'don't walk backwards like a ninny and fall into potholes – please just move forward like a normal person, and don't look back until I say so. Come away up!'

Dodging the ruts, endeavouring to ensure safe footing in the dark, they clamber up the Maclaggan Street gully and through Serpentine Avenue. It is hard work and just as Billie gasps that she is quite out of breath, they arrive at the Canongate junction. There are no gaslights up here; the night air is clear and crisp. The gully's sides have blocked a good part of the northern sky and they have avoided looking south.

Until this moment, when she turns at Robbie's command.

All pretence drops away. 'Oh! How wondrous! Not just the glow, but all the colours, even reflecting in the harbour – and all the ships outlined! I have seen the Lights often, but never so clearly and vibrant as this. Such a splendid sight – yes, it is like magic. You have convinced me. Pinks and blues! Blues and greens and oranges – oh, it's gone, but wait! There's a bright purple – and now it's green again, Robbie! Such a brilliant green!'

'Emerald,' claims Robbie.

'And cobalt! And sapphire like the Queen's jewels!' Billie is overcome by the vision.

'Look, now they're turning red – ruby!'

'Turquoise! And amethyst!'

'Tangerine!'

'You can't say that – it's not a mineral!' She glares triumphantly.

Tiger eye quartz, just like your eyes. A surge of desire engulfs him. He is glad of the darkness so that she, his quaint little sister-friend, cannot notice his burning face or his tautening body.

'You win,' he says quietly.

Without warning Billie's eyes fill. 'Oh, Robbie, I don't feel like I'm winning. I've been feeling so very sad. I cannot reconcile that Mr Northey has not come home to us, even now. It is not real, but it is. I have been so awfully unhappy. It all seems so strange that he won't be here to see me matriculate.' She draws a quivering breath. 'And also, I have missed seeing you too since you've had your head down at varsity. I've felt very lonely, somehow. But look! Now the Lights seems to be saying something to me, something that makes me a wee bit happy again. Is that a bad thing, do you think?'

'No, it isn't bad,' replies Robbie, 'and you will no doubt be sad off-and-on for a long time to come. And yes, the Lights are so splendid. I knew this presentation which I ordered especially – ' he creates an expansive gesture across the panorama, ' – would cheer you up. But Miss Frost, you are shivering in the chill that bears your name. You are so small and young, and I am so tall and old, ho ho! Shall I draw you in closer and tuck your little arm into mine so that you may become warmer?'

The aurora swirls its splendour across the evening sky. 'I don't mind,' she says, too casually.

CHAPTER
THIRTY-EIGHT

Meg is still unconvinced. It is over a year since she and Alf were informed of the bequest. Although Mr Ogilvy urged them to proceed with caution until probate was finalised, there have been no challenges from Edwin Northey's mother who inherited the Dunedin estate, nor from his sisters' husbands who now own substantial holdings on the Taieri Plains. Meanwhile Alton has apparently not risen from his cups. Nobody has ever questioned the possibility of another slice of inheritance, for which James Ogilvy is cautiously pleased. The five thousand pounds are, therefore, waiting for the Maguires in the Bank of New Zealand.

But to purchase their own home on the back of such misfortune? It doesn't seem proper to Meg, even if Alf is of a different opinion.

Her old friend, Nessie, in whom she has confided obliquely, is also encouraging. 'Well, dearie, I canna see what the problem is. If I had an auld aunty who left me a for-tune, God rest her soul, I'd nae look that gift horse in the mooth. I'd be buying a wee hoose as quick as a flash. Think, Meggy, think about your future. Och, it will be more secure for ye, what with the likelihood of yon Abbeyleix being sold again to another owner, and ye having to negotiate to stay on. Much better for all of ye. Aye. So what say take a wee leuk-out soon?'

Modest housing is at a premium in Dunedin town. Tours of inspection are made but each time Meg turns down the property due to some supposed deficiency in size, con-dition, price or location. And she most definitely will not move far from the area that has been her life since arriving in the colony as a young bride back in the late 'forties. There is far more choice in the city outskirts but although she has a friend south in the Caversham borough, another north at Kaikorai and even a few down the peninsula at Portobello, Meg is adamantly opposed to the notion. For what would they do with acres of land or having to walk for miles at their age? How difficult would it be for Billie to get about to school and Ogilvys and such-like? No, indeed, close to the city and Maclaggan Street it must be. And while her bones ache by the end of the day, she enjoys her work at the Abbeyleix with the ability to fall straight into bed after she closes the kitchen for the night.

So, should their current situation come to an end, then will be the time to consider the next step. Meg is not inclined to be moved on the matter and Alf knows better than to press her. He will merely keep watch over the situation in his own quiet way.

Billie exits the doorway of Ogilvy and Ogilvy after her day's attendance and turns for home. She is known to many on the street and young men are starting to doff their hats. Her pert face is taking on more mature contours and starting to catch up with her wide eyes. Some would say she is becoming quite handsome, in an odd sort of way.

This day, her balance receives a jolt as she spots her nemesis lounging nonchalantly against a building diagonally opposite. She has managed to avoid him for over a year, but how will she do so now without turning back uphill and heading the long way home?

The nefarious Tinks Toomey knows her timetable; nothing is by chance. Nor has he been idle on other counts. He is a born negotiator and nothing pleases him more than calculating a deal. Missing out on an opportunity or being beaten at his game provokes him to an inward seethe of anger, but he negotiates his way through resistance on most occasions.

'I'll tell ye what,' he will entice a hesitant customer, 'I'd not want to t'ink of ye missin' out on an opportunity, so here's what I'll do for ye, and 'tis it between us, and nobody else. Sure, but ye have me in yer hands entirely.'

Tinks can charm the birds out of the trees or a consent out of a rejection, just as his father and his father's father did, leaving only a blur of doubt in the recipient's mind. His dress is always stylish and he keeps his boots polished. He is gaining a respectable reputation in some quarters. Not for him, in and out of gaol like his drunken sod of a Da, not for him the need to mash in a woman's head to get cooperation. No, he may carry a flick knife for protection, but it is charm that carries the day.

This day Billie decides to continue down the hill, endeavouring to ignore him.

But he calls out, 'Miss Billie Frost! Hey, Miss Billie! How are ye on such a grand afternoon? Sure, you're lookin' gorgeous in dat bonnet.'

Miss Billie? Tinks has never addressed her anything other than Bill. And here he is – one moment across the road and now right upon her – bowing pretentiously.

'Miss Billie, I just saw you comin' and t'ought to meself, 'tis time to speak wit' ye. Time to put misunderstandin' behind us, if ye know what I mean?'

'Misunderstanding? I don't think so, Mr Toomey. I understood exactly what you proposed and you – you disgust me!'

'Miss Billie – Bill – I'm desprit sorry about dat time. Sure, I got da wrong end of t'ings entirely, and I humbly apologise.' He executes a contrite stance.

She does not smile or change her stiff expression. 'Thank you, but stay away from me. You give me the shivers and I don't want to think about it.'

But as she marches away she cannot stop thinking about him. Thinking of the line of his jaw, the curve of his mouth. Thinking of his scent.

CHAPTER
THIRTY-NINE

November 1874

The second year's interest on investments has been deposited into the Thornbury Trust account and at sixteen, Billie is permitted to use it on her own behalf. She could buy more books for Miss Clayton's class, or clothes, or something grand for Meg and Alf. But she needs a better idea: a project. Preferably something that involves making money and helping others. Like helping her school friend, Temperance Ivimey.

Tempe finished her schooling last year and assists her mother at dressmaking. Maude Ivimey is now a widow and works exceedingly long hours towards the upkeep of her home and while the house is secure, there are always expenses to be paid and repairs to be made. With Tempe executing fine beadwork and cut-work trims, their clientele is becoming more exclusive and no longer do they need to labour quite so hard for meagre rewards.

Some women bring yards of fine cloth sourced from France or Italy – the sturdy weaves produced by the local woollen mills are not for them. Others make their purchases at Ross and Glendining, general importers, or have bolts sent out from Home. Whatever the source, these patrons require high-quality garments and they pay well. The dressmakers can hardly keep up with demand. Billie's friend Susannah – recently returned from the wilds of Central Otago – has been introduced to the Ivimeys. With her willowy body, she acts as a muse and patrons regularly fall in love with the beautifully draped effects.

Billie has compiled a few of her sketches based on fashion plates from *The Ladies' Gazette of Fashion* from London and *Harper's Bazaar* which she now orders direct from New York. She drools over the etchings.

'Listen to this, how grand it sounds: *"Ladies' promenade dresses! Sea-side and watering-place costumes! Street and indoor toilettes!"* And see the description of fabrics: *"camel's hair brocaded wool ... green silk shot with chestnut ... ruby chenille with inserts of embroidered taffeta."*

'And look at this darling cape: *"a mantelet of ecru cashmere lined with sapphire silk moire and pleated matching trim."* Oh, if only we could make some up for a display!' she finally looks up from the magazine.

'If only we had a small salon,' muses the widow, 'we could move this jumble and have our parlour back. What heaven it would be to actually sit upon one's own chaise without being surrounded by a workroom.'

The seed of an idea bursts open. 'Yes, that is the answer!' declares Billie impetuously. 'We shall have a salon!'

Maude Ivimey smiles. How amusing this girl's notions always are.

James Ogilvy is circumspect.

'It is a matter of return on investment, my dear. Indeed, it is your money and as each year goes by you shall receive another three thousand pounds, or thereabouts, being interest on your capital. This will remain in trust, but you may apply for it on an annual basis from now on. However you must be canny – as I am sure you will be,' he adds, at pains not to patronise. 'So what we must do is work out the projected income versus projected expenses – and risk.'

A frisson darts through Billie's mind at the concept of risk and increases her determination to take it.

Maude Ivimey has been confidentially informed of the Thornbury Trust and its connection to Billie, but it is some time before she can come to terms with the whole idea. To lease a shop is one thing – and as a married woman, she may do so under the law – but to have the setup paid for by a child is another. Yet, rational thoughts allow her to see it as an opportunity to develop a business that, with hard work, could provide a more certain future.

With a great deal of reflection, documentation, and caution that it would not do to put all one's eggs in a single basket, James Ogilvy releases one thousand pounds into the venture. A ten-percent gross profit is to be strived for by the end of the first working year and the accounts will be closely scrutinised. Space is leased in a brand-new building on George Street. It is ideal in both size and position.

The only exterior adornment is a golden insignia, *Ivimey*. Billie had proposed *House of Ivimey* but Mrs Ivimey felt uncomfortable – too pretentious – this is Dunedin, not Paris! And her patron agrees the single name looks splendid. 'No need for fussy detail,' she states, unanimously appointed as the promoter. 'All we need now is one glorious model in each of the two front windows and "By appointment only" on the door. I do believe that it may be quite a success!'

It is indeed unique. A shop front – *a couture salon!* – with daring displays is a new thing in Dunedin and draws attention without the need to advertise. Word of mouth is the best thing and the orders steadily increase, requiring the employment of five more accomplished workers including Billie's old school friends Sophia and Ellen, and two more sewing machines. Treadles and fingers seldom rest.

Whatever the details of dressmaking – innovative design, skilled cutting, meticulous stitching – James cautions Billie against being involved in the day-to-day running of the business. 'Too many cooks, etcetera, my dear. I would urge you to stand well back from anything other than concept and promotion.'

Concept and promotion! Just what she enjoys – not

tedious details like costing and calculating. With three mornings now being spent as a student teacher for Miss Clayton at Arthur Street School, and one day with Mr Ogilvy, plus her newly defined role with Ivimey, her head whirls. But it is a good whirl, she thinks.

She strolls through the Botanic Gardens with Susannah. They are stylishly over-attired, and although their costumes are frail, their resolve is strong. It is a lovely place for a mild Sunday afternoon and Susannah has brought the picnic basket while Billie contributes the rug. Formal rose beds are coming into bloom and flax specimens glow against the deeper foliage of the rhododendron dell. Although the imported trees are attractive, Billie feels more affinity with the native plants and tries to entice her friend to explore further up the hill.

'No, thanks,' says Susannah. 'If I want native bush it's freely available up the back of our land – Father's continually chopping at it. And besides, I've had enough exercise today. I vote we spread out here by the creek.'

The picnic and warmth produces a profound sense of inertia. They shed propriety to loosen their stays, lie back on the tartan rug and relax.

He leans closer. She cannot move. Her face is glowing and her lips are parting. The pull of her eyes to his is increasing. She is melting, melding deeply into the earth. Her lips are parting, and she wants him. She wants his kiss. She wants to sink into his skin. She wants his touch and his passion. He is holding her down but he will not take her yet. She is craving him and she is urging him. But then – he is drifting away without looking back. Tinks has gone.

Susannah is prodding her. 'Billie! Billie, wake up! Whatever are you moaning about? Are you ill? I think you've had too much sun – you look exceedingly flushed. You should do up your bodice and become calm. I think we should pack up and start for home.'

Billie gathers herself together, but the dream has set her body on fire and her thoughts into tumult.

CHAPTER FORTY

She cannot forget it, cannot let it be. She seeks him out and suggests he walk with her next Sunday afternoon, ostensibly to view Ivimey salon's grand window displays. 'There's nothing like it in the whole of Dunedin,' she boasts.

Tinks is amused; he is used to such female games. *Bill, ye t'inks ye're a lady, but ye're a whore at heart.*

She demonstrates the cut of the fanlights, the sheen of the signage, the grandeur of the slowly revolving mannequins. Then on to the quality of their garments: 'And just look at the costumes, so sleek and soft, a tiny petticoat just showing beneath – all so lovely.' She droops her head and eyes, then slowly lifts them to Tinks' face. Their bodies are close and their breaths blend.

But Tinks does not kiss her. Then, as if nothing had come between them, he pulls out his pocket watch. 'Four o'clock, is it? Well, I'd better be off, so.'

And as he swaggers down the dusty road, her senses course after him.

The weeks pass and all the ruses she can muster will not summon him to appear. She can smell him, she can envisage him, she can thrill to his enigmatic charm. Tinks seems impervious; he knows the effect of nonchalance.

Billie cannot concentrate at home, or at work. Meg cannot comprehend why the girl has left her library book in the fowl house and the eggs in the privy. Mr Ogilvy has occasion to reprimand her over misfiled papers. On one occasion, she walks on past the Law Courts as he turns in, leaving him to stare at her receding form. On another she leaves papers behind. 'Are you in a dream, girlie? This is not correct procedure. Please focus on the task at hand.'

But focusing is impossible. She is in a state of being, and her mind is elsewhere.

At last she encounters Tinks – he has contrived the meeting to suit himself. They stroll up the Rise. They admire the harbour view.

Soon, without obvious greed, he traces a finger through her hair and it loosens. She lifts her hand to his and he guides her close. Clasps her around the waist and tilts her backwards in a sham swoon. And then pulls her upright and close to his face, his hard blue eyes penetrating hers. Their lips part, and for a few long seconds only the heat of their skin betrays life.

Then he tosses her aside. 'Ah, ye're gorgeous, Bill, but I'm not good enough for ye. Not good enough a-tall.' And as she reaches for him in confusion, he turns away saying, ''Tis best we leave it, so.'

It is a long, brooding walk home for Billie. She is con-
fused. She is piqued. She wants Tinks, and by crikey she
shall have him! But no – what does she care? He is a vain
idiot. She shall ignore him when he next tries to interest
her.

CHAPTER
FORTY-ONE

February 1875

The sun's rays sparkle on the bevelled windows of Ivimey, and the displays are alive with reflected light. Three young ladies survey the effect.

'It's just super,' says Susannah.

'Super,' agrees Temperance.

'Super and marvellous!' cries Billie. 'But – ' then she scowls '– there is something wrong with those *Harper's* models.'

The girls gaze past the solitary mannequin in each of the twin partitions, and up to the fashion plates suspended from the ceilings with imperceptible threads. The full-page prints have been carefully eased from the magazine and glued lightly onto black baize, giving them the appearance of being captured in floating frames.

'Maybe they are too plain? Do they need a coloured edge?' suggests Tempe.

'Certainly not, Tempie – they need to be neutral against the gorgeous dresses on the mannequins. Neutral but also eye-catching. Oh, now I know what it is with the *Harpers* plates! The models look so – so stiff! That's it – just look at that lady resting her arm on a mantelpiece and looking so bored! Where is the movement, where is the excitement? For if they have such beautiful clothes, why are they so stiff?'

'I daresay the artist spent many long hours with the models to get every detail correct,' says the pragmatic Susannah.

'Yes, I suppose. But I have an idea – our own mannequins could be made to move! On a thingumajig on the floor.'

'A revolving plinth?' suggests Tempe.

'Yes – oh, my dears, how lucky we are to have such brains between us!' laughs Billie as they move into the salon. 'Alf will be able to help; he still loves to do make things. We shall have a plinth that will turn as by clockwork, and I'll ask him to make one immediately!'

'Immediately,' Tempe mouths at Susannah. They silently agree that their friend is behaving quite oddly.

'All we must do is get our patrons through the door into the salon,' Billie continues, 'and I have such ideas from reading these. It's done in Paris and New York. They have models walking up and down, not resting on a silly mantelpiece! They have fashion parades each season in the Paris salons, so phooey, why shouldn't we do it in Dunedin?'

'Er, because – ' Susannah is becoming dazed.

'We need to work on a whole collection, not just bespoke orders. And Susie, you would be wonderful as the head model!'

As the trio returns to the inner sanctum, Maude Ivimey descends from the workroom with a partially made gown. It is a beautiful, modern creation of lustrous silk – lilac shot with dove-grey – subtle and deceptively simple, and even more so when slipped onto the padded dressmaker's form to await the client's fitting.

Tempe says, 'What fun Mama, Billie says we shall have a fashion parade as soon as we have a collection ready.'

'Very good, my dears, very good,' is the indulgent response.

Billie squints at an illustration in a *Harper's* magazine 'You know, those little hats are adorable, but the models have all that hair, so stuffed up and twisted into shape. Crowning glory, phooey! I shall implore my models to chop it off!'

'Chop it off indeed – what young lady in her right mind would chop off her hair?' This time the proprietor is alarmed.

'I would – and I'll show you!' Billie grabs a pair of dress-making shears and yanks her mane out an angle.

'Stop, stop! You silly girl! Whatever would Mrs Maguire say?'

Billie's hand freezes. The last thing she wants to do is cause Mother Meg any more sorrow. 'Just joking, dinna fesh,' she cries, the expression reminding her of Robbie. She veers back to the topic of short hair. 'But one day I *shall* cut my hair. I shall wear a beret and carry a little dog with a plaid jacket onto the omnibus and it will be so fashionable and marvellous!'

Maude Ivimey is extremely concerned. Is the child – she always thinks of her as a child – is she all right in the head? Granted, she has always been a bit fey. But now she seems more erratic. Even volatile.

It is the last time she will see Billie so animated.

CHAPTER FORTY-TWO

The vow to ignore him is weaker than the pull she feels. Billie breaks her resolve and seeks out Tinks. She prattles about the weather. He affects boredom. Then she expresses her interest in visiting the Botanic Gardens with a handsome, elegant companion – perhaps he would care to be that person? He says he will consider it. How Billie dislikes herself for pursuing him in this way, but he'll see. She *will* tame him.

Safely away from home territory, she twists up her hair, pinches her cheeks, and rubs her lips with geranium petals before she meets him by the Leith.

With affected indifference they stroll alongside the stream and onto the estate. They pass lovers and families. They admire the flowers. They eat plump strawberries and

tiny sandwiches from the tearooms, and taste champagne
that he has procured with a nod and a wink.

After two hours, Tinks has lightened himself of at least
three shillings, and considers this sufficient foreplay. ''Tis
about time you repaid me kindness, Bill.'

'Fancy suggesting that to a lady, you tosser!'

'Tosser, is it? And what might ye be yerself?'

'Oh, Tinks, I'm enjoying this so. You're a wild one for
sure, but such good fun!' And Billie whirls away.

His eyes are dangerous and his breath heavy. He must
control himself for a while yet. And so it plays out – a little
more champagne, a little more teasing. Now they are well up
the hill, away from afternoon strollers.

'I think I feel a little dizzy. Help me down, Tinks – the
ground is dry enough.'

'If I lay ye down, Bill, what might people suppose if dey
chance by? Sure, I'll start standing up t'anks. Now release
yer bodice, if ye please.'

This time Billie cocks her head in a tease. 'I won't!' she
says.

'You won't, is it?'

'What do you take me for, sir?'

'I take you for a tormenter, Bill.'

'Surely not!'

'Surely so. Come here to me now.'

Like a wave surging on a dangerous tide, the forces col-
lide. There is no teasing now, no mocking, no game. He
thrusts and she bites, and it is intense and powerful. Aban-

donment without care of the consequence. It is a turmoil of urgency, angry and raw.

And when it is spent and he pulls away, there is no intimacy. There is no tenderness.

CHAPTER
FORTY-THREE

James Ogilvy is perplexed. Miss Billie has always expressed a love of walking past the gothic-inspired First Church on their way to and from the court on Wednesdays. Block upon block of creamy Oamaru limestone set against Port Chalmers basalt, built with great delicacy of detail incorporating many turrets and pinnacles, a massive rose window and a soaring spire – these features have previously enchanted her. But today she suddenly says she is bored by architecture and bored by walking to court and bored by being a teacher's assistant. So be it, thinks Ogilvy, she is probably – well, she is growing and probably becoming – ahem. He shall ignore her moods for the while.

Meg is more than perplexed. She is at her wits' end about Billie's emotional stability. Since the death of dear Mr Northey over a year ago the child has been low and sad, then frenzied with the establishing of Ivimey, then suddenly coy and secretive. And now haunted and restless. She must address the situation tonight.

When the kitchen is closed but for herself, and Alf is on his usual stool in the private bar, Meg decides it is time for action. She relaxes her corsets and pours two mugs of warm milk and bids Billie to come. 'Sit with me, darling child. Sit with Meggy by the range, and tell her what's the matter.'

Without warning, tears swell and torrent from Billie's eyes. There are very few times that Meg has ever witnessed such an event – spurts of fury or joy maybe, but not such an outpouring of anguish. 'There-there, my love. There-there. Whatever is it, my darling one?'

As when she swayed the tiny mite, as when she consoled the little girl with bloodied knees, Meg pulls Billie onto her wide lap and strokes and rocks and kisses her tears. 'Whatever is it? It can never be that bad, my little pigeon.' Which moves Billie to the next stage and now she is shuddering and gasping. 'There-there. There-there,' Meg croons.

'Mother,' gasps Billie, 'Mother, Mother. My little mama who died for me!'

Meg believes she understands: the blockade the child built around herself after the terrible night that claimed their dear Eveline is at last being torn asunder. After all those years of being a brave little one, and latterly the grief being brought back to her with the death of Mr Northey, the poor girl is at last releasing her pain.

Meg gently encourages, 'That's it, let it go, child, let it go. Cry for your mama and take comfort that her soul is with God.'

'No-no-no!' shrieks Billie wildly. 'It isn't Mama's soul – it's that I've let her down! Let you and Alf down! Let myself down! Been so foolish – oh, oh!'

Meg gently slaps the hysterical cheek. 'Stop it at once. You are being ever so silly and getting yourself into such a state. Now stop it, I say!' And as her child's body slowly relaxes from its harsh shudders: 'So tell me properly, what is amiss?'

Billie finds it difficult to put it all into words. To tell Mother Meg how that charmer had mesmerised her, as a weasel does a rabbit by its circular snare. To admit how her loathing turned into longing.

She confesses her tale of persuasion, passion, daring. How she and Tinks toyed with each other, how she urged him on, behaved like a coquette. How the secret risk was so thrilling; how she then craved him; how they came together in a hunger.

'Well, my love,' says Meg after the flood abates, 'mesmerised is as mesmerised does. You're that in your own way – and like attracts like, whatever the price. And who am I to say I'm disappointed in you? I can see you're more disappointed in yourself than anything I could say. But I've heard it all before – it's a story as old as the hills. Yes, mark my words, many have gone before you, many higher and many lower, drawn into the arms of an enchanter. Thinking the fireworks would stay up in the sky. Yes, thinking that giving themselves to a man would mean a jot when it doesn't. At least, not to *that* sort of rotter.'

As her ward's eyes brim again, she cautions, 'Ah, my

poor lamb, my poor brave little lamb, you must not take on so, or you will make yourself quite ill.'

'But, Mother, there is more I haven't yet told you.'

Meg tries to breathe steadily, although her heart is pounding with anxiety at what is to come next.

'Mother, I couldn't stop myself wanting to be with him. I thought I could make him happy and I tried to meet him again. But he was so moody. And then last week he cut me dead in the street! Looked right through me as if I were nothing – as if I were worthless. All of a sudden I realised he isn't worth a hoot, to treat me like that. And now I despise him like I used to do. He's a blot, I've been a fool – and now I'm a destroyed woman!'

'Nothing of the sort, indeed. Don't make it worse by being overdramatic. Delusion is behind you now, and you shall forget it all, eventually. Unless – '

In a moment of dread laced with impeccable restraint, Meg reaches out to touch Billie's belly.

'But no – thank the Lord, thank the Lord, indeed.' Meg has related the predicament to Alf after they climb the wooden hill and lie spooning in their narrow bed, as they have done since their early married days. 'And we must hope and pray it is the end of the matter.'

Alf is rigid with anger. It is not the end of the matter as far as he is concerned.

With the release of her woes, Billie becomes more clear-headed. At Meg's insistence and under the pretext of having a frightful cold, she has taken some time away from tutoring at Miss Clayton's school, where her beloved mentor has become Mrs Julius Vogel. She has taken time away from her Wednesday work with James Ogilvy and also from Ivimey. And now she is feeling stronger. 'Have gumption, get on with life,' Billie instructs herself.

And in the manner that has seen her through a life of chance, Billie gets on with it. She directs her focus on Ivimey which is buzzing with industry. New ideas are starting to flow but she tempers them with a new perception. There is nothing in New Zealand to compare with the concept of fashion parades, although she has heard of private showings by Kirkcaldies in Wellington. Yes, she might go to Wellington next year. There is much to think about, much to be done.

She is strong and resolute again. And when the day comes that little old Mungo dies peacefully in his doggy sleep, she clings to his little body for a whole day, but after a splendid wake, Billie Frost smiles down on him and soldiers on.

CHAPTER
FORTY-FOUR

June 1875

'There are those who fight a duel over a lady's honour,' says Robbie Macandrew – who in the fullness of time has grown into an assured young fellow and a junior associate in his father's office. He has taken time to plan, and this is the moment of truth.

Tinks Toomey curls his lip. 'She's no lady, boyo!'

Robbie disregards the jibe. 'And there are those who fight it out in the streets.'

'Over a whore? What a desprit idea!'

'And – ' as if still not hearing the braggart speak, '– there are those who are found beside the gasworks with a neat gash to the head. He must have stumbled and hit it.'

Tinks' colour starts to fade. Bejasus – the toff means it. He knows this one, the cyclist friend of Billie Frost, now working in his Da's office. How very convenient. Scottish to boot, full of themselves and their education. He spits onto the dirt, carefully missing the challenger's boots.

Two other young men move towards the tableau in support of their leader, who continues.

'And then again there is the occasional one – lower than a snake, lower than a worm, lower than the most nauseating cockroach – who's found on the rocks below Lawyers Head. Och, aye, the puir man, he must have wanted to end it all and jumped over the cliff.'

Tinks is silent.

'You get my drift, man?' The tone rises slightly.

Tinks stares ahead, calculating his chances, fearful now.

'And so, to avoid any of the above, my friends – ' Robbie cocks his head at his men, '– and I strongly recommend that you scarper. Vamoose. Leave town, and never, ever return.'

No response.

'Do I make myself clear, Mr Toomey?'

Tinks manages a nod, but his eyes swivel.

'I canna hear you. What is it that you are telling me, man?'

The Irishman makes a slight move, but before he has time to draw his knife the bodyguards pounce. One circles his neck in a beefy vice while the other twists an arm hard up his back until he ejects a curse-laced yelp of pain. Pressure is eased but as soon as Tinks Toomey moves, it is reemployed.

Eased again, he starts to regain poise. 'I was headin' off

288

anyways. Likely to Australia. I'll be leavin' evench-ly – like in a few days.'

'A few days? No, sir – by then a man will have washed up on the rocks.' Robbie's voice is harsh.

'I will, I will, I'll be off tomorra den.' Tinks' face is pasty now.

As if he hadn't heard, Robbie continues, 'Nothing will please me more than to see such a carcass on the rocks.'

'I'll be gone, so.'

'That's the spirit!' And with a pistol at his back under cover of good companions with arms around each other, Tinks Toomey is ridden out of Dunedin town, over the plains, over the ranges, and deposited without food or transport well out of harm's way.

As the horsemen drop their hostage amongst the high outcrops and whirl away to start their long canter back to Dunedin, one laughs his dire farewell to the terrified man: 'Die of thirst or freeze to death, whichever takes your fancy!'

Alf's emotions have been running high. He is aghast that his darling girl would have even thought of running off with that illiterate waster, and furious that the sod would touch her. He had taken a chance on calling upon young Mr Macandrew. It might have been the wrong move, but it has been a gauge of the man's true character.

He has now witnessed the gang-press from a doorway, held back only by a solemn pledge that he would not cut the blackguard's throat himself. Retribution has been met, and he is satisfied.

The operation's commander releases his clenched hands and breathes in deeply. Slowly – calmly now – he lets it out. It is done. And nothing else would have done, other than to avenge the honour of Billie Frost.

CHAPTER
FORTY-FIVE

The following winter, the Southern Lights play across the sky in bold counterpoint to the softly floating Milky Way. Robbie Macandrew watches the awesome performance with Billie by his side. He has had his supper again at the Abbeyleix, now under the proud ownership of the Maguires. He is well set up in town in an agreeable flat during the working week, but he enjoys the humble comforts of the hotel's kitchen. Meg is always welcoming and Alf smiles knowingly.

Robbie looks down on the young woman. 'I do believe Vogel's vision is making us a better country, Frostie,' he says. 'We have more immigrants these days, more new settlers, and many capitalists like Father to help with employing the labour. Aye, I daresay it will come at a price, and I have no doubt things will dip again soon, especially if the world economy does. But we certainly are forging ahead,' he nods firmly.

'Gold has established our wealth, but gold runs out. We are so far away, down here at the bottom of the globe, yet I believe we are well off here by the standards of our parents at the same age, with plenty for all if certain parties up north would only stop fighting over it. I know there are poor and rich in New Zealand now too, but generally it is so much more egalitarian than the old country. It's comforting to know we, here, are the new breed.'

Robbie's confidence is not without foundation. With his studies completed and his feet on the first rungs of his father's business, he believes his future is bright.

'We? You really believe we are of a new breed?' Billie's face turns up at her tall companion.

'Yes – you and me, people of our own generation who have grown up with expectations. I can plan my future so much more than I could have in Scotland, and with Father's position and investments up Central he has built up more than he could ever have dreamed of.

'Not that he discusses it with me, of course,' Robbie assures, 'but I'd say we are well set up. Aye, we were modestly well off in Scotland, but in New Zealand we have a different sort of freedom. The railways are expanding in all directions. Education is soon to be free and secular. Everything is growing so fast! This is indeed a bonnie country.'

Then he shudders. 'Och, it's nippy! Let's come away inside – I certainly need a wee dram in my tea now, and no doubt you might have one too. Just to warm up, mind!'

They shiver themselves into the cosy kitchen alcove that is known as 'Meg's corner', and they draw deeply on the aroma from their mugs.

'I do enjoy it when you talk of the future, Robbie. I feel you really want to include me – that is, in an easy way. What I mean is,' she ponders, 'dear Mr Northey had a stiff manner, and Mr Ogilvy has a more learned one when he talks to me. And Alf has always encouraged me to explore my ideas. But once you start talking – not that you do very much – I get a feeling of – I can't explain it.'

'I may not talk nonstop like you, but you are part of my thoughts from time to time.'

'And you mine, you great galoot.' She is awkward now.

'You would speak to your elder in such a common way?'

'Elder, tosh. What is elder or younger anyway? Only –' And Billie's mind returns to the lunacy she was previously drawn into.

'Only?'

'Only I can't get over being such a fool. Nobody would want to marry me after that – that *thing* last year. Of course I do want to go on with the fashion business, keep building it up – and oh, wouldn't it be so wonderful to go on to be really successful!' Her countenance falls. 'But, Robbie, I am undone, ruined as a woman, and shall have to become an old maid. I've completely spoiled my chances to become a wife.'

'Frostie, you are the silliest girl I ever came across. But also the most – the most daring, the most – the loveliest,' he concludes quietly, his senses racing. 'In fact, while I dinna wish to suggest I am lovely, we are very similar, you and I, in many ways. Yes, you are bold and independent and I dare-say you shall become a captain of industry before any other woman in New Zealand, with your growing empire! But I do believe we complement each other – ' his voice wavers, then recovers '– even though I am a boring old bachelor and you are an astonishing young lady.'

'You are such a beautiful liar! But I may never be able to live up to your beliefs, not now, thinking of what happened with that – that Blot.'

He stiffens. 'That Blot will not trouble you again, lassie, not if I have anything to do with it.' His voice is as cold now, cold as his heart against the man who lured this girl to the edge of reason. Then it softens, 'Never mind: "A fool doth think himself to be wise, but a wise man knows himself to be a fool" – or so some fool said.'

'Shakespeare, *As you Like It*,' responds Billie.

'And,' Robbie gains courage, 'would you be fool enough to marry – one day, that is?'

'I would only marry if a man were to love me in spite of everything – and that would eliminate most.'

He will not let her dwell on it. 'Since Shakespeare seems to be popular tonight, how about this one: "I would not wish any companion in the world but you".'

'The lovers in *The Tempest* and – ' Her voice tapers off.

Silence now, wrapped in the kitchen's warmth, as Billie slowly comprehends, slowly caresses the truth of what she has always known in her heart.

Until Robbie speaks. 'Why are you gawking at me that

way? Your mouth is gaping – you do look rather foolish! Never mind, I'll away now. But if the Lights play again tomorrow, shall we again gaze at them together down by the harbour? It shall be my birthday treat for you, Miss Frost!'

CHAPTER FORTY-SIX

1st September 1876

The Lights do play again the next evening. Shards of emerald and crimson, curtains of purple and gold – the symphony pulses lustily across the heavens. To the twosome on the quay gaining double pleasure from the water's reflection, their only response is silence.

Then, as if the force penetrates his own body, he draws her close. He knows she is headstrong and wilful, that she will not be tamed, that she will forge her own path. And he knows that he loves this wild, courageous girl.

Slowly he releases her and tilts her chin high. 'I asked something of you yesterday, in my clumsy way. So tonight, now that you are the grand old age of eighteen and with the Lights playing so well, I shall ask you again properly: Miss Frost, would you consent to – '

'Oh, yes, I would, darling Robbie! I would, I would!'

'Good lord! Can a man not ask the most important question of his life properly without interruption?' He will brook no further response and his lips seal down onto hers, firm and unforgiving.

She breathes in his essence, deep and long. He is so much a part of her own being, so different, yet so equivalent. He applauds her without indulgence, and rebukes her without rancor – and oh, how she adores him!

Finally, he speaks. 'And so, at last: will you be my own love?'

'I will,' whispers Billie. And then she slants her eyes in that familiar golden challenge: 'but – there is one proviso.'

Robbie groans through a dagger of fear. 'Indeed – and what is that?'

'That I may be foolish occasionally, and that you may always be wise – well, most of the time!'

He swoops her up high and she is silhouetted against the glowing sky. Their laughter suspends for a moment in the bracing night air, and then it echoes across the harbour, ripe with joy and promise.

ACKNOWLEDGEMENTS

With thanks to the NZ Society of Authors (PEN NZ Inc) for assistance given through the CompleteMS programme; to Lesley Marshall for her fine eye; and to Martin Taylor for his expert judgement. To my parents Tom and Joyce Jory who unwittingly triggered my desire to find out about Maclaggan Street. And especially to my family and friends who encouraged me in writing this novel.

In researching the back story for *Southern Gold*, I am indebted to the following sources of information:

Built in Dunedin: historic buildings and their stories
First Church Heritage Centre
Hocken Collections, University of Otago Library
National Library of NZ, Papers Past
Queenstown and District Historical Society
Te Ara Encyclopedia of New Zealand
Toitu Otago Settlers Museum

And for further insights:

Barmaids, Billiards, Nobblers and Rat-Pits: Pub Life in Goldrush Dunedin 1861–85. Hargreaves, R.P. Dunedin: Otago Heritage Books, 1992

Bright Fine Gold: Stories of the New Zealand Goldfields. Heinz, W.F. Wellington: Reed, 1975

Old Coaching Days in Otago and Southland. Lovell-Smith, E.M. Christchurch: Capper Press, 1976

Pubs Galore: History of Dunedin Hotels 1848–1984. Tod, Frank. Dunedin: Dunedin Historical Publications, 1984

Southern People: A Dictionary of Otago Southland Biography. Dunedin: Longacre Press, 1998

Station Life in New Zealand. Barker, Lady Mary Anne. First published MacMillan & Co, 1883

Wanted, a Beautiful Barmaid: Women Behind the Bar in New Zealand 1830–1976. Upton, Susan. Wellington: Victoria University Press, 2013

ABOUT THE AUTHOR

Jude Thomas lives in New Zealand on the beautiful Mahurangi Peninsula north of Auckland. Born and raised in Dunedin, she was expressly forbidden by her parents to go near the Maclaggan Street area. This finally gave her the encouragement to dig into its colourful past and start writing about  it. She also spent many summers in the Central Otago region and says she can still smell the wild thyme and feel the shimmering heat. But her lasting memory of a southern upbringing is the piercing winter and her intensely itchy chilblains.

Jude is a member of NZ Society of Authors (PEN NZ Inc) and the International Writers' Workshop NZ Inc. In 2015 she was awarded a manuscript assessment through the NZ Society of Authors CompleteMS Programme, which is supported by Creative New Zealand. This has been invaluable to Jude in the writing of *Southern Gold*, her first full-length novel. Website: judethomasauthor.com

9 780473 365554